Love Without Hope

Love Without Hope

Wally K Daly

BBC Books

To Don Webb with thanks.

BYKER GROVE is a
Zenith North Production

Published by BBC Books,
a division of BBC Enterprises Limited,
Woodlands, 80 Wood Lane, London W12 0TT

First published 1991

ISBN 0 563 36261 8

Set in Baskerville by Redwood Press Limited, Melksham, Wiltshire
Printed and bound in Great Britain by Clays Ltd, St Ives plc.
Cover printed by Clays Ltd, St Ives plc.

CHAPTER ONE

Speedy was in big trouble. He was still only fifteen, but was now fairly sure he wouldn't be around to enjoy his sixteenth birthday. He knew his fingers were bleeding, could see blood trickling down his wrists, which the rain constantly lashing down failed to remove. But he couldn't feel any pain. He couldn't let them leave the fingertip hold they had for one second and look at them, because if he had done so he would have crashed to his death in the canyon, hundreds of metres below. The only thing that was holding him, flat and frightened against the sheer wall of the mountain he was clinging to was the tips of those bleeding fingers, and the tiny crevice his toes had found on the narrow ledge of rock which provided the only foothold on the granite face. In spite of his terror he knew he had to keep edging slowly round the mountain to the sharp corner some metres to his left, around which corner was the reason for him finding himself in such a predicament on this dreadful rain lashed night.

A young woman was trapped on the self-same ledge of rock, and screaming not only for help, but screaming for him by name. Slowly, but surely he made progress, then, when only half a metre from his goal, disaster struck.

A patch of rock crumbled beneath his toes, and his legs were flying free. Now, hanging only by his fingertips, feeling that at any second his arms would be pulled from their sockets, he was swinging freely over the abyss, and screaming with pain and terror. He knew he mustn't look down, the first and golden rule, he must not look down; but he couldn't stop himself.

The drop appeared endless; what had seemed only hundreds of metres when he set out, was now on second view thousands. Lightning ripped the sky, and lit the canyon far below revealing the jagged razor sharp ridge of rock that promised a cruel death should he be forced to let go his precarious hold.

Just at that moment, the moment he thought he could hold no longer, but must surely plunge to his doom, the cry which had brought him on this mad pursuit in the first place came once again, from the other side of the mountain:

'Speedy! Help me! I'm going to fall!'

The cry gave him the strength to try one more time – and finally his scrabbling feet found a foothold and his legs stopped their mad swinging, and soon he was pushing himself onward once more.

Now the cry was growing more insistent:

'Speedy! help me! I'm going to fall!'

And he went on as quickly as he dared, inch by painful inch.

He finally reached the corner. And now a truly terrifying and testing moment presented itself. He had to lift his left foot off the narrow ledge that was holding him, stretch it round the other side of the ridge, and blindly find a new foothold. His foot was searching but there was no foothold to be found. He brought it back and pushing his head into the howling gale, squinted around the corner, and saw who called.

It was Charlie. To Speedy the most beautiful girl in Byker Grove. Older than him by a few months, but he didn't care. She was wonderful, and she needed his help. She was standing bare foot on a slightly wider ledge than he had so far found, splayed with her back to the mountain, her long blonde hair whipping away in the wind, her hands behind her desperately clinging to small finger holds she had found. The rain pouring down had soaked the thin nightdress she was wearing, transparent it clung to her every curve, and as she stood there the tears pouring she called his name over and over, desperately pleading for his help.

Speedy saw that he would have to swing his legs around the corner, if he was to reach the ledge on which she stood, and having taken a deep breath to steady his nerves which were screaming with fear, he swung them and leapt, letting go his hold as he did so, and shifting his body in the same direction immediately searching for another finger hold.

For seconds he kiltered on the edge and then having found his footing, and a crevice for his fingers to grip once more, he was safe on her side of the mountain.

'I'm coming Charlie!' He screamed against the howling gale which now gusted even more furiously and tried to pull him off the ledge as if angry with his achievement of surviving so long against such heavy odds. 'I'm coming!'

She turned and looked in his direction, her face terror-stricken. 'Quickly, Speedy! I'm going to fall!'

But her last words were drowned by a vicious pulsating new noise, that grew louder by the second. As Speedy slowly looked to see where the deafening new sound came from, a helicopter slipped into view above his head. A rope ladder hung swinging from its base, and someone was quickly climbing down the ladder from the body of the craft, presumably to be in a position to rescue them, and help them climb aboard.

Speedy's joy that they would both now be saved was short-lived, as lightning flashed once more, he saw that it was Robert on the ladder, and Speedy felt, without knowing why, that he wouldn't be included in the rescue.

In seconds the helicopter was hovering above the point where Charlie stood crying with relief, and Robert, now level with her, was helping her onto the ladder, and then keeping behind her protectively as they both climbed hand over hand to the safety of the helicopter's cabin above.

Speedy howled against the ever increasing gale. 'Robert! What about me!'

Robert didn't look round, simply carried on upward and then reaching the top helped Charlie to climb safely aboard. Immediately he started winching the ladder up after him.

Once more Speedy screamed out: 'Robert! What about me!'

And Robert for the first time looked at him and smiled his most charming smile before shouting above the noise of the blades and the gusting wind, 'Sorry, Speedy! No room for two!'

And with that the door was being closed, the helicopter lifting, and in seconds it disappeared back over the cliff face, taking its mind-numbing noise with it, and Speedy was left alone in the darkness once more.

'No,' Speedy said quietly. 'No.'

He too turned so his back was to the mountain, hands splayed behind him. 'No.' And at that second, as thunder cracked directly above, a bolt of lightning struck the ledge beneath his feet, and it crumbled away and Speedy was plummeting downward. This time he shouted it. 'No!!'

As he fell at ever increasing speed his body slowly curved over as if in a dive, and his head finally led the way, and he could clearly see the jagged razor sharp rock below that spelt his doom, rapidly growing larger as he approached.

One final scream: '*NOOOO!!!*' and instead of landing a broken wreck on the rocks, he was awake and sitting up, face drenched with perspiration, in his tiny bedroom at the Gallaghers'.

His breath was coming in gasps, his hands shaking with fear, pyjamas soaked with sweat, clung to him the way Charlie's gown had clung in his nightmare. He found it hard to believe, as it had been so real, that was what it had been, just a nightmare. Just one of many that had been haunting him for weeks. Dawn light was breaking, and in its glow he saw the handle of the door turn. The door swung open and Robert was standing there looking at him with a slightly quizzical look on his face. Speedy lay back down again, not wanting to look at this man who had only minutes before left him to die on the face of a gale lashed mountain. Robert entered the room and crossed to stare down at him.

'You all right?'

'Fine,' came Speedy's curt reply.

'You called out.'

Speedy couldn't bear to continue the conversation, angry that Robert of all people should be intruding on his thoughts at this moment, when he needed room to think this thing through.

'I said I'm fine!'

Robert continued to look at him for a little while, then crossed back to the open door. Speedy's call stopped him.

'Robert!'

He turned back to look at Speedy who by now was sitting up once more.

'Sorry. Didn't mean to be so rude.'

'That's all right.' Robert leaned against the edge of the door hoping to take some of the weight off his aching legs.

'You got a problem, Speedy?'

There was a defensive edge in Speedy's voice as he replied.

'How do you mean?'

'You've been a bit . . . edgy, lately. Not like you. You have a problem?'

Speedy smiled inside, rueful. Thinking to himself, 'Robert, if you only knew.'

But instead of saying it, and thereby going dangerously near to the truth, he ducked it.

'It's nowt. Just not sleeping too well. Nightmares.'

'Want to talk about it?'

If only I could, he thought. *If only I could. But I can't Robert. Especially not with you.*

'There's nothing to talk about. They'll go soon enough.'

'Suit yourself.'

And with that Robert went back through the door, closing it behind him.

A moment, then Speedy lay back down, thoughtful. Another moment, and he turned to the small cupboard beside his bed, and from under a pile of magazines picked up a photograph. He held it so the dawn light fell on it.

It was a photograph of Charlie with her boyfriend, Robert.

Speedy looked at the photograph for a long time, before finding the courage to say what had to be said. Finally he found the courage. 'I love you, Charlie.'

At the precise moment that Speedy spoke the words, Donna was contemplating a problem that was the very reverse of his. Speedy suffered nightmares that had such clarity as to appear to be reality. Whereas Donna was in the situation of the stuff that nightmares are made, but knew it was for real.

As she had sat through the long night hours with Lisa at the Outpatients of the local teaching hospital, she had played the nightmare's opening scene over and over in her mind's eye, wishing she could wake and find it wasn't true. But it was.

The argument between her and Lisa, her stepmother, had started after the pub had closed and Jim had locked up for the night. They were in the downstairs bar. A remark from Lisa on Donna's late arrival home had simply been a spark to the touch paper, and Donna had become the cracker that exploded.

Thinking back to it, Donna couldn't remember any given part of the argument with any clarity, simply that being Donna she knew she would have been cutting, cruel, and vicious, the verbal boot going in unremittingly whenever an opportunity presented itself. But what she could clearly remember was her dad's horror-stricken face, aghast in the realisation that the two women in his life could hate each other so much.

Jim had stood near the bar and watched the pair of them like a spectator at a tennis match. His head shifting backwards and forwards between them as they each took their turn at screaming abuse at the other.

Donna had been aware that his face was going whiter and whiter as the argument continued, until finally his lips were a tight pink gash against his pallor. She had no idea at that time it was anything but the vicious argument that was affecting him, in fact felt strangely pleased that he was finally getting the message, that Donna thought it was the biggest mistake of his life marrying this awful, awful woman, who, for all her pretty, blonde, butter-wouldn't-melt-in-her-mouth saccharine sweetness, was just a street fighter at bottom, who when the chips were down could give as good as she got, but Donna could always give better.

Donna had no idea it was anything but the argument, until he quietly said, 'No.' It wasn't 'No – you must stop this argument.' It was 'No' as if responding to, and rejecting, something that was being said inside.

Both Donna and Lisa knew it was serious, the fighting instantly stopped as they looked to him, eyes tight closed as if against an immense inner pain, swaying where he stood. What happened next Donna remembered as if seen in slow motion. Though in reality both she and Lisa had rushed to try to save him and failed to get there in time.

Jim had simply keeled over backwards. Without bending or putting out his arms to break his fall, he had slowly keeled over and his head collided with the brass foot rail that ran around the bottom of the bar with a sickening thud, and a gush of blood immediately gouted from the massive gash on the back of his head. As Donna dashed to hold him to her, she realised that she could hear screaming, loud, terrified screaming. Lisa had run straight to the telephone behind the bar and was dialling nine-nine-nine so it couldn't be her.

It was seconds before Donna realised it was she herself who was screaming. From the telephone Lisa bawled:

'Shut up, Donna!' Shocked, she did so.

'Put this on the cut to try to stop the flow!'

Lisa threw her a fresh teacloth from the linen pile near the telephone. Donna made it into a pad and did as asked. Without meaning to look she did, and her stomach turned. The cut was massive, already there was a pool of blood that spread and stained the floor.

'Dad, Dad?!' No reply. As Lisa started speaking urgently into the telephone, Donna wondered if she would ever hear him speak again.

That was hours ago. Now as dawn broke and unseen, daylight spilled into a new morning, she simply sat beside Lisa waiting for doctors to pronounce their verdict. She realised Lisa was looking at her, and turned to face her coolly. They had spoken hardly a word all night, both knowing that the other was guilty of bringing this tragedy down on them.

It was Lisa who finally broke the strained silence, speaking quite gently, offering the chance of a truce.

'Why don't you go home, Donna? Get some sleep?'

But Donna wasn't yet ready for a truce by any means.

'I've stuck with it this far – I'll see it through. Besides – when he comes to, he'll be asking for me.'

Pleased she watched Lisa's reaction to the remark. Lisa now knew that Donna thought that, without a doubt, though Jim had married Lisa, his true affection still lay with Donna his only daughter.

Donna's satisfaction would have been short-lived if she could have seen her father in 'crash', the room in hospital Accident and Emergency departments where all cases in serious risk of dying are rushed to upon arrival at hospital. He was wired to a monitor that lazily flicked the graph of his heartbeat onto its screen. Half a dozen black suckers were on his chest, two more on his temples, their threadlike tails trailed away to where they were wired to the appropriate equipment. Drip tubes were in his arm and nose, and Jim, deathly white lay un-responding as doctors and nurses fought to bring him back from the brink of death.

Meanwhile at the Gallaghers', in the room next to where

Speedy lay still musing over his sleeping problem, Fraser was up and about and ready for an early start. He headed as quietly as he could via the kitchen to the front door collecting his bike from the hall on the way. He'd made it as far as the front gate and was about to mount when he heard a bedroom window above open. He looked up and there was the red-haired peril – his younger sister Spuggie.

'Where you off to, Fraser!'

In spite of himself he had to smile, all his efforts to get on his way without waking the household had immediately been blown by Loudmouth.

'I've got to go let Geoff know I can't help him this morning.'

He was about to get on the bike when the next question came.

'Why?'

Fraser put off getting on the bike, knowing that the chances were that once the questions were underway they would come like bullets. They did.

'I'm going to our flat.'

'What about school?'

'Off site day.'

'What you going to the flat for?'

'To clean it up a bit.'

'Why?'

'Spuggie, you're sounding like a record!'

Deciding he'd given her quite enough answers for one morning, Fraser finally mounted his bike and pedalled off, calling over his shoulder as he went, 'See ya, Spuggie!'

Spuggie watched him go, her face slightly troubled. She'd got a distinct feeling something was going on. What she didn't know yet, but sure as anything she intended to have it out of him finally.

Closing the window she quickly finished dressing and headed for the kitchen. As she entered a morose Speedy was just sitting down at the table. Even though he hadn't been exactly sociable for days she decided to test the waters.

'You're early today.'

The quick scowl he threw in her direction made her realise she need not have wasted her breath.

'No chance of sleeping while you're bawling out of the window at Fraser, now is there?' As Spuggie crossed to sit at the table opposite him, he got the cereal packet and shook it over his bowl, and discovered it was empty.

'Was that you?'

She knew well enough what he meant but wasn't set to make it easier for him.

In seconds the spat was underway.

'Was what me?'

'Had the last of the stuff and didn't get the new packet out.'

'You've just watched me come in. I haven't had owt yet.'

'When's that brother of yours going to get some manners.'

'If you've got owt to say about Fraser, say it to him. No business of mine.'

With a *Humph* of temper, Spuggie angrily stood and headed for the door, thinking she could do without the aggravation at that time in the morning. As she reached the door she paused, throwing her comment at him from there.

'I don't know if anyone's told you yet, Speedy, but lately you've become nothing but a great big miserable pain in the bum.'

Lou, the warm and motherly foster mother to them all, was about to enter, weighed down with a fresh load of clean clothes, through the same door that Spuggie was intent on leaving by, and made the comment in passing.

'Enough. Go get ready,' she said.

As Spuggie went off to the bathroom, Lou continued into the room heading to drop the clothes off in the corner, speaking as she did so.

'Not put in the most ladylike of manners, Speedy – but I've got to admit Spuggie's got a point. Maybe it's time you got it off your chest?'

'You could be right, Lou. I've got to talk to someone about it soon or I'll bust.'

'Coffee?'

The word coming out of the blue startled Donna awake. Not that she'd been properly asleep, staring blankly ahead, dulled by the monotony of the endless wait she had been in a sort of half trance. Hoping that Lisa hadn't noticed, she effortlessly found a suitable Donna-ish wide-awake reply.

'If I have any more I'll puke.'

Then her frustration at their predicament struck home and she stood to let it pour angrily out.

'Why doesn't somebody come and tell us what's going on?'

Lisa tried to calm her.

'They said they'd have further tests to do after the X-rays . . .'

And failed.

'That was hours ago! He could be dead and gone by now for all we know!'

Lisa stood to face her, equally angry that Donna could voice her own fear so exactly.

'Don't say that! You hear me?! Don't you dare to say that! Don't even dare think it!'

At which the door to the waiting area swung open and the white-coated figure of the young doctor in charge of the case was there looking at them. Hearing the door open, as one, Donna and Lisa had swung their heads around to look in that direction. There was a long pause before he spoke.

'Mrs Bell?'

'Yes,' said Lisa, a slight quiver in her voice.

'I wonder if you'd both come through to my office.'

As they walked the corridors to his office, Donna decided she truly hated hospitals. They were too brightly lit, too hot, too full of alien smells, too full of stretchers being wheeled around with lifeless bodies on them, simply too full of general nastiness. When they finally arrived at their destination, one glance decided Donna that the doctor's office was also the pits. Papers everywhere, assorted items of clothing scattered around as if he was using it to live in, which indeed he was at the moment, as the hospital was short-staffed and his shifts were endless. He'd already been on duty for the last twenty-seven hours and was shattered, but Donna wasn't to know that. He had to clear some clothes off the two chairs in front of his desk so he could make space for them to sit.

When they finally did so, he went behind the desk, and lay the brown folder which he was carrying on it, sat down, opened it.

Lisa and Donna simply watched him tensely. It seemed to be forever before he spoke, but when he did it was dynamite.

'It's confirmed Mr Bell sustained a fracture of the skull when he collapsed.'

They had no comment, both knowing from his tone there was more to come. Finally it did.

'During our tests, we also discovered why he collapsed in the first place, and I am afraid it is not very good news. In fact – it's very bad news indeed.'

Lou poured Speedy's cereal from the new box she'd got from the cupboard, then poured the milk on as well. Speedy knew he was being spoilt, and Lou knew that even when they feel quite grown up, it's sometimes good to treat the youngsters in your care like kids. You never know what might come from it. She didn't have long to wait. Speedy decided to get it off his chest.

'It's something that's been going on for weeks now, Lou. Getting to the point where I'm almost afraid of falling asleep, I just know it'll happen again.'

She knew it was important not to rush it, and just probed at it gently.

'What will?'

His spoon stirred the flakes in his plate as he thought about it. Finally finding the words he let them go.

'I have these most ... incredibly vivid dreams, really nice, always with someone I'm really ...'

The word that had leapt to his mind was love, but suddenly he was afraid that Lou might laugh at the thought of Speedy being in love. He knew she wouldn't really but still found a substitute word.

'Always someone I'm really fond of. Someone I really like. And then – just as I'm dreaming it – something horrible always happens to spoil it at the end.'

The look on Lou's face was gentle. This could perhaps be the start of a conversation she had had with many of her other charges in the past.

'In what way does it get spoilt, Speedy?'

It was proving a much harder conversation to get off the ground than Speedy had anticipated.

'It's very hard to talk about it, Lou.'

Lou realised she was right. A subject that had often come up with young men over her years as a foster mother. But it still needed delicate handling.

'Speedy, over the years there's been dozens of boys lived here, and I've learnt a lot. Now there is a very natural stage when boys reach puberty, when dreams can be used by nature to ease the pressure.'

Speedy was slightly bemused by what Lou was saying. She was speaking as if she knew what was going on, but what she was saying bore no relationship to his nightmares. As she continued to speak he continued to try to fathom what she was getting at.

'The sort of dream I'm talking about, Speedy, makes most young boys feel bad, but it shouldn't. Those sort of dreams, and what happens, is the most natural thing in the world and nothing to be ashamed of.'

And finally he'd worked out what she was talking about, and chuckled inside at the thought. If that was the problem there would be no problem. He decided to put Lou right.

'No, not that sort of a dream, Lou. I know what you mean, and you're right, they're really freaky; but the sort of dream *I'm* talking about is where you fancy a girl, really fancy her; and her boyfriend ... '

Speedy stopped talking abruptly, as the door opened and Robert walked in. Lou didn't press him to continue, just watched Robert cross to sit with him at the table, as Speedy finally started eating.

'Got over your nightmare yet?'

'Yeh. I got over it.'

And watching from the sidelines Lou suddenly realised that Robert, who had been Speedy's hero for months, no longer held that lofty position, and wondered why.

There was a long low wall around the hospital car park, and the car park was just a few metres from the entrance to the hospital. It was there that both Donna and Lisa sat quietly, shell-shocked at the news the doctor had so recently given them.

As Donna sat, the doctor's words whirled and wheeled in her mind.

As well as his fractured skull, Jim, it turned out, was suffering from 'renal failure', a medical definition that meant both his kidneys were now dead, and there was very little chance that they would ever function again.

Donna had the doctor spell out the implications. Yes – he would be on a dialysis machine for life; no – they were unlikely to suggest a kidney transplant in the short term; yes – it would be difficult to find a match as his blood group was extremely rare.

Both Donna and Lisa now sat quietly and thought their thoughts. It was Donna who finally broke the silence, and the question came almost as an accusation.

'You knew he was a diabetic?'

The doctor had said that occasionally diabetes could be a 'causal factor' in renal failure. Donna had argued her father wasn't a diabetic, the doctor said he was, and knew it. But did Lisa?

'Yes. I knew. He was diagnosed some months back.'

Donna felt an immense sense of betrayal, she was his daughter, he should have told her as well.

'Why wasn't I told?'

Lisa pondered long before she spoke, she knew well how delicate the situation was. She and Jim had talked long and hard about whether he should tell Donna or not. It had been his decision not to. The decision of a loving father. Donna, he believed, could do without the additional worry of his health intruding into her childhood.

Lisa finally got her words together.

'Jim thought you'd had enough heartache for a while. Thought it best you weren't told.'

Donna was stung by this confirmation of the betrayal. She had thought she came first in his life.

'But he didn't mind telling you.'

'I'm his wife, Donna.'

'And I'm his daughter!'

Suddenly Donna realised she was very near to tears.

'I won't allow it. I won't allow Dad to be tied to a machine, a cripple for life. I just won't.'

'How can you possibly stop it, Donna? How can you possibly stop it?'

'I'll find a way! Just you wait and see! I'll find a way.'

And finally, having fought successfully for so long, Donna lost the battle with her emotions, and cried.

At the same moment that Donna let her tears fall, on the landing at the Dobsons', Debbie also was near to tears, but if they came, they would be tears of sheer frustration and anger. She banged on the bathroom door in an absolute fury. Jemma had managed to beat her to it yet again, and Debbie was desperate.

'Will you hurry up, Jemma, I've got to go!'

But no reply was forthcoming.

'Jemma!!'

But all of Debbie's continued shouting was to no avail.

If she could have seen what Jemma was getting up to in there, she wouldn't have been so surprised at the lack of a response.

Jemma was busily putting a large blob of cotton wool in her right ear. She already had one sticking out of the left, a floppy incongruity.

When she had successfully pressed the large blob into her right ear, she stood back to admire the result, quite pleased. She thought she looked a bit like a bunny rabbit, even though that wasn't the intention.

Having finished checking that they were well in place, she crossed to open the bathroom door all ready to face an irate Debbie, who called one last time as the door started to open.

'Jemma! Open up!'

And miracle of miracles Jemma finally opened it.

'You took long enough!'

Jemma screwed her face up trying to work out what was being said to her, but couldn't quite manage it.

'What?'

'I said ...' And then, amazed, Debbie realised why Jemma wasn't hearing her.

'You've got cotton wool in your ears!'

Jemma shook her head.

'Sorry can't hear you – I've got cotton wool in me ears.'

Blank-faced, bemused, Debbie watched Jemma walk off towards the kitchen, and didn't see her gran coming from the bedroom behind her and immediately popping into the bathroom. It was the slamming of the door and the click of the lock, that finally made her realise what had happened.

'No, Gran! I've got to go!'

But too late.

In the kitchen, silence sat heavily, Alan, Kath, and Nicola had been 'having words' yet again, but enough words had finally been said to silence all three of them. Now they continued to eat in silence, thinking their separate thoughts.

Nicola thought her mum and dad's constant going on about the company she had recently kept, and the dangers those alleged friends had got her involved in, would finally drive her potty. While Alan and Kath, individually, simply feared the message wasn't sinking in. If they only knew it, they needn't have worried. Their message had sunk in with a vengeance.

Nicola had vowed to herself that she was going to make very sure that anyone she made friends with from now on, would be squeaky clean, and not the sort who attracted the attention of the police. The last few weeks, she had decided, had been an unfortunate phase in her life that she was very glad to have put behind her, and certainly didn't intend to repeat.

Jemma said her cheery greeting as she arrived in a slightly louder voice than she normally would have used, in an attempt to hear herself.

'Morning all!!'

Jemma watched her mum's mouth moving as she spoke without looking up, trying to understand what she was saying.

'Get a move on, Jemma, you're going to be late.'

Then decided that she'd understood clearly enough.

'It was nothing – Debbie just wanted to get into the bathroom that's all.'

Kath, a bit thrown by the strange reply, looked up as she spoke. 'What?'

Jemma got that one straight off.

'Hot? No – I feel fine.'

As Jemma crossed to sit down at her place at the table opposite Nicola, Kath watched her amazed and dumbstruck. Alan spoke for her.

'Jemma?'

Without showing any sign of having heard Jemma leaned over for the packet of flakes and started to pour them onto her plate.

Nicola glanced at Jemma, and then she too did a double-take. As Jemma put the packet back down on the table and got the milk jug, Alan tried again to get through using a notch more voice, just this side of bawling.

'Jemma!'

And succeeded in attracting her attention.

Jemma paused in her pouring.

'Yes, Dad?'

'What are you playing at now?'

Jemma strained but couldn't manage to fathom what he was saying.

'What?'

Alan's patience was suddenly wearing thin.

'I said . . . why have you got cotton wool in your ears?'

Jemma realised that though she was trying very hard, she was simply not understanding.

'Naw. It's no good, Dad – I can't hear you – I've got cotton wool in me ears.'

Nicola immediately half stood and leant over the table grabbing at the cotton wool blobs as she spoke.

'Well, we'll soon sort that out, won't we!' As she grabbed both and pulled them out of Jemma's ears, Jemma gave a cry of protest and pain.

'Oo! That hurt!'

And Kath was once more back in the conversation.

'Don't be so rough, Nicola.'

'Just wondered what she's playing at, that's all.' Nicola said in her defence. Jemma immediately stood and snatched the cotton wool back out of Nicola's grip.

'Give me them back! You'll spoil it!'

And having got both pieces, stuck them firmly back in her ears again as Alan spoke.

'Spoil what?'

Realising her dad had spoken Jemma turned to him once more.

'Sorry, Dad. Can't hear you. Cotton wool.' And another not too unusual morning in the Dobson household continued on its way.

Geoff arrived at the Grove early, and was looking forward to his cup of coffee with Alison and Fraser when they arrived. As Fraser had an off site day from school, he'd promised to come in and give a hand with a few hours of humping, to sort out some heavy gear that wanted stacking out of the way in the basement.

Geoff got out of the car, slammed it shut, and crossed to unlock the front door, and was soon picking the mail up off the floor. As usual no personal letters but lots of brown envelopes that spelled yet more bills. As he put them on the side table intent on opening them later, he sensed a whisper of noise high above in the upper rooms of the club. His shoulders tensed and he listened intently. There it was again. He made for the stairs and started walking up them with a light tread. If there was anyone there they would be turfed forthwith.

Slowly but surely Geoff went ever higher in the club, pausing to quietly open doors and check each room on each landing he reached. At one point he thought he heard a noise that indicated that the door leading to the outside turret at the very top of the old house had been opened, but decided it could have been his imagination playing tricks. 'Anyway, soon find out.' He thought to himself. This was as he was climbing up the final narrow twisting staircase that led to that very door. Reaching it he found it was unbolted. The night before he had made sure that it was locked.

Geoff opened it slowly, and as he did so the daylight flooded in. He stepped out onto the flat roof, high above the Byker grounds, he looked around and to his surprise, saw that there was no one there.

He didn't look up at the roof of the main building; if he had done he might just have seen that behind one of the chimneys, the prowler hid in wait. Intent on getting Geoff.

Instead Geoff looked down over the waist-high battlements

and watched as Alison drove up to park her car alongside his. As she got out of her car he called her name.

She looked up squinting into the sunlight, and there was the unmistakable shape of Geoff etched against the skyline. She called loudly enough to carry above the slight breeze.

'What you doing up there, Geoff!'

He called back equally loudly.

'Thought I heard someone prowling about!'

And then, Alison was aghast to see there was indeed a prowler. The man had appeared behind Geoff as he called, and that man was now furtively approaching Geoff with his hands held out in front of him. His hands were heading for Geoff's shoulders, and the clear intention was that Geoff was going to be pushed off the roof of Byker Grove to a certain death in the courtyard below!

CHAPTER TWO

The Byker Grove bunch were either on their way, or in the case of Jemma and Debbie about to be on their way, by a variety of means to their various schools throughout the Newcastle area.

Some biked it, some bussed it, some tubed it and some hoofed it, their paths occasionally criss-crossing as they went on their way, but all were on the move, apart, that is, from Jemma and Debbie.

Debbie stood on the doorstep adamant that she wasn't going to walk with Jemma while she still had cotton wool sticking out of both her ears. It was bad enough having to go with her in any case, it really cramped Debbie's style when any good-looking lads were around, Jemma took the mickey if she attempted even to flutter a lash, but now Debbie really put her foot down. When it came to going with her while she was looking so unutterably stupid, she had no hesitation in letting Jemma know it was just not on.

'Look – if you think I'm going to walk with you while you're looking like that you've got another think coming.'

The trouble was it wasn't as if the message was getting through.

A blank 'What?' was all that Jemma could manage for the hundredth time.

Debbie stood there on the step and had a slight sisterly freakout.

'Jemma! You are driving me potty!'

Jemma watched as Debbie spoke while jumping up and down with hardly contained fury, with her head cocked to one side quizzically.

'Naw. No good, Debbie. Can't make a word out.' Suddenly Jemma's eyes brightened, and her face came alive with a beaming smile.

Under Debbie's gesticulating hands, she'd spotted Angel and her younger brother coming along the street in front of the house. Angel was Jemma's latest and greatest friend. She was pretty, and a good laugh, but best of all she had a head of hair that was so amazing that Jemma reckoned it made even

Spuggie's red mountain look quite ordinary. Angel's was thick, long and blonde, and the dozens of ribbons that Angel's Irish mum bound tiny strands of it with on bath nights, while Angel's hair was still wet, gave it a gorgeous crinkly look.

It was no surprise to Jemma, but a big one to Debbie, that Angel and her brother also had cotton wool blobs sticking out of their ears which waggled up and down in unison as they walked.

'Oh great! Angel and the shrimp! I'll walk in with them. See you, Deb!'

And then, much to Debbie's relief, Jemma crossed to join the two of them as they passed. Debbie listened to snips of the crazy conversation as they both walked off beside the silent boy.

'How's it going, Angel?'

'You what?'

'How's it going so far!?'

'Oh great, Jemma! How's it going with you?'

'What did you say, Angel?'

'How's it going?!'

'Oh smashing. I'm really getting up Nicola's nose.'

'You what?'

'It doesn't matter!'

'Whose getting fatter?'

'You what?'

And in spite of herself, Debbie had to laugh.

By coincidence Debbie's laugh coincided with Alison's scream, as she saw the silhouetted man about to push Geoff off the roof of Byker Grove. As is often the way, the scream carried words with it.

'Geoff!' Behind you!!'

As Geoff swung round in alarm, the hands grabbed his shoulders.

'Got ya!!'

And momentarily Geoff's heart leapt and his pulse raced. Momentarily, because he saw it was a smiling Fraser who had grabbed him and given him his shock.

'If you ever do anything as stupid as that again, Fraser! . . .'

He let the threat hang in the air, as he noticed Fraser's sadness at the rebuke for what he considered to be a simple gag. Geoff went on a different tack.

'There's me chasing prowlers and you playing silly beggars.'

Fraser's eyes went owl-like behind his glasses.

'Prowlers?'

Geoff explained.

'Thought I heard something – no one here.'

Then Fraser smiled again.

'It was me.'

'You?'

'That's right. Found a puddle from last night's storm in one of the rooms. Thought I'd come and check out the guttering. Bad crack up there that needs sorting.'

Geoff's eyes followed Fraser's pointing finger. Fraser was indicating where he had been, the highest sweep of the Byker roof. Geoff turned back to look at Fraser.

'You went up there?'

Fraser nodded his agreement.

Geoff's face clouded with restrained anger.

'Don't ever do owt as daft as that again – not by yourself, right?'

'But . . . !'

Geoff wasn't interested in hearing any arguments.

'No buts. I know what our insurance covers and what it doesn't, and it doesn't cover foolishness. Got that?'

Fraser had the grace to hang his head a little.

'Yes, Geoff. I've got it.'

Satisfied Geoff decided once more to let it go.

'Okay. Let's go see your puddle.'

Geoff gave an assuring wave to Alison still below and looking up anxiously. He called out the one word.

'Fraser!'

And relieved she waved back and headed for the front door.

Geoff's face dropped a mile when he and Fraser finally arrived at the room where the rain had penetrated. Not only was there a pool of water but the plasterwork was soaking. He spoke his thoughts quite glumly.

'Now that we can do without. Let's hope it can be patched.'

Fraser was quite hopeful of the chances.

'Should be able to do it. Have a go at it tomorrow, shall we?'

Geoff didn't miss the fact that Fraser was set on putting it off.

'Why not today?'

Fraser smiled.

'Got a favour to ask. I want to go off and sort the flat out.'

The flat, which was where Fraser and Spuggie used to live before their mother had been taken into care, had been empty for weeks. Geoff couldn't understand the sudden need to get it sorted in a rush.

'So what's the big hurry to get it done today?'

Fraser was quite pleased to tell him and get it off his chest. He hadn't told anyone else as he didn't want it to get back to Spuggie until what was to happen was confirmed.

'I went to see Mam last week – and it's looking good.'

Fraser's mother had had a drink problem that had got seriously out of hand after their dad, who also was a boozer, had stormed off and left them a few months back.

She'd drunk so much she finally couldn't eat, and almost starved and drunk herself to death, before her condition was finally spotted by the GP after Fraser and Spuggie called him in. Fraser remembered how she looked when she was first taken into hospital – dreadful. And then, as they slowly built her strength up, how much better she'd started to look. Then they had suggested, while staying in the hospital, that she should go on the 'Alcoholics Rehab' course, to get her off the drink and keep her there for good. Fraser had been to see her there a few days back, and thought she looked great. Almost like the mam he used to know before she got ill. He decided to share his pleasure with Geoff.

'They said failing a relapse she could be home any time – it's up to her now. She only has to say the word and she's out – wouldn't want her to come back and find the place looking a tip. You know?'

And of course Geoff did.

'You get another off site day tomorrow?'

'Yeh.'

'Okay, you push off and get the flat done today, but eight-thirty on the dot tomorrow morning back here, right? Got to get that leak sorted out soon or we'll be asking for wet rot as well.'

Fraser had been pretty sure that Geoff would let him take the time off, but was still pleased to have it confirmed.

'No problem about getting here on time. See you then.'

As he headed for the door Geoff called.

'Don't you want a mug of coffee before you go?'

'I'll organise one at the flat.'

And Geoff watched him go, pleased that his luck as regards his mother was changing finally.

Speedy was strolling along with PJ who wasn't making a very sympathetic audience this morning.

When Speedy had told him about how rude Spuggie had been at breakfast, calling him a pain in the backside, Speedy had got a quick and unexpected response from PJ.

'Well, you've got to admit she's got a point. You haven't exactly been the cheeriest person in the world lately.'

In the face of the confirmation that he had been a bit of a pain lately, Speedy looked for an excuse. He hadn't realised his misery and bad temper of the last few weeks had been quite so obvious. As he thought about it, in the distance he spotted Winston and Duncan who were on the opposite side of the street and heading in their direction. Having got his excuse together he tried it out on PJ.

'I'm just a bit shattered that's all – not sleeping well.'

And out of the blue came a bombshell. Instead of sympathising, PJ's face was suddenly wreathed in smiles the way it always did when he was about to tell a gag. When he spoke Speedy couldn't believe he was hearing it.

'I am. And it's great. I dreamt about Charlie last night . . . '

Charlie! His secret love Charlie being dreamt about by PJ! He just couldn't believe it.

'You what?'

PJ put on a smile before speaking as if to a child.

'No, no, Speedy. You're supposed to say "Did you?" '

Speedy couldn't work out what was going on.

'What do you mean?'

PJ spoke even more slowly to keep up with Speedy's present intellect which didn't seem very bright.

'Let's start again – 'I dreamt about Charlie last night' ... Now you give the reply.'

Hesitantly Speedy gave it.

'Did you?'

'No – she wouldn't let me.'

PJ was immediately falling about in a paroxysm of laughter, pausing mid laugh to confirm Speedy had understood the gag.

'Get it? It's a gag. "Did you? No – she wouldn't let me." ' And then he continued his manic laughter once more.

Speedy, white with anger, felt a cold tight knot of fury building in his stomach like a fist. He was so incensed at the insult to his loved one that he felt he couldn't stop himself but punch PJ right in his laughing face. To avoid doing so, he had to quickly turn and walk away. PJ was bemused that Speedy was walking off instead of falling about laughing. Couldn't work it out. He called after him.

'Hey, what's the matter? Just a joke!'

And Speedy called back over his shoulder in a voice shaking with anger.

'I don't find it funny!'

As PJ, wide-mouthed, watched Speedy continue on his way, Duncan and Winston who had now drawn level having seen the drama played out, crossed the road to join him.

'So, what's with Speedy? Bawling out and going off in a huff?'

PJ simply shook his head in disbelief before replying to Winston's question.

'Who knows, Winston, who knows? Come to think of it, who cares? Spuggie's right, Speedy's nothing but a pain these days.'

He stopped watching Speedy's disappearing back and went for a change of subject.

'Okay, Duncan, how goes the fund?'

Since their friend Gill had died in the car crash, they'd all been racking their brains to get money to buy a memorial to his memory. Duncan was the fund's present treasurer. His one word comment didn't come as much of a surprise to PJ.

'Pathetic.'

Winston wasn't prepared to leave it at that. Gill had been his best mate, and he'd been there when he died.

'If we're really going to get this memorial finally – we're going have to start getting our act together and raising some real money.'

PJ smiled his smile.

'Funny you should say that, Winston. I think I've got the perfect scheme for making a fortune.'

Duncan knew PJ's plans from old. So his voice carried a touch of scepticism.

'Like what?'

But PJ had decided to go for a bit of mystery.

'Byker – tonight; committee room; all to be revealed.'

And with a cheery 'See you,' PJ was off on the same route as Speedy had taken.

While Winston and Duncan also continued on their way, trying to guess what crazy scheme PJ had in mind this time.

When Fraser arrived at the flat and opened the door the smell of the place hit him right up his nose. It ponged.

Automatically on entering he had called out, 'Mam!', but then smiled at himself for working on automatic pilot like that, his mam he knew was safe in hospital.

Fraser wasted no time in thinking about what a pigsty the place was, but just got on with it. Having opened all the windows to get air moving through, he emptied the fridge and the bread bin, removed dead fruit from the bowl, putting it all into the black bag in the kitchen bin that was already half full of rotting waste. Then he humped it down to the dustbin area, and dumped it.

Then it was the turn to sort the pile of filthy dishes in the kitchen sink. He went to the carrier bag he had brought with him, took out the teabags, sugar and milk he'd bought, and then found what he was looking for, washing-up liquid.

He ran the tap, and the water splashed back at him as it hit the overflowing crockery. On the back of the door he noticed his mam's pinny, and decided to put it on. He knew he would look daft but who cared, and who would see him in any case?

And then he simply settled down to the serious business of trying to clear the sink of its filthy load of crockery and utensils, with the thought uppermost in his mind: 'What a way to spend an off site day.'

Nicola was also off site. She had done some work after everybody had gone off to school and work, but she was soon pretty fed up with her own company so decided to go to hear the latest scandal from Donna.

Arriving at the pub where Donna lived with her dad and stepmother, she found that the place was fairly chaotic and full with everybody going on loudly about an accident someone had had. She crossed to the bar behind which Lisa was on the telephone speaking animatedly. Nicola decided to hang on there while Lisa finished the one-sided call, trying to work out as Lisa spoke what it could be about.

'It's important I talk to her ... Yes, you said – but she must have left some forwarding address ... Look if she contacts you – could you tell her to ring Lisa Bell, urgent.'

And with that Lisa put down the telephone and turned and saw Nicola.

'Thank goodness you've arrived, Nicola. You're just the person to talk to Donna at the moment. Go up and see her, she's really upset.'

Not more boyfriend trouble, Nicola thought to herself, but she didn't say it, just gave Lisa the chance to say it herself.

'Upset?'

But instead of confirming Nicola's first thought, she dropped a bombshell instead.

'Jim's had an accident.'

'What's happened?'

'Go up and let Donna tell you, Nicola, I'd better get these customers sorted out.'

Lying on her bed in the clothes she'd been wearing the night before, Donna knew she must look dreadful. Her eyes she imagined would be red-rimmed, her face streaked with last night's mascara running in black trails down her cheeks, but she just couldn't stop the tears, couldn't get herself together enough to go and do something about her appearance. Every time she nearly managed to stop, a picture would come into her mind of her dad falling and cracking his skull, or the doctor at the hospital breaking the news, and either picture would immediately set her off in floods again. She knew she must look dreadful, but didn't realise quite how dreadful she looked, until Nicola came in and looked at her aghast. Even though she didn't say it, Donna knew it from the look in her face, and once more the tears flowed.

Nicola crossed to sit on the bed beside her, taking her in a friendly hold.

'What is it? What is it, Donna?'

It was a long time before Donna could get the words out, but finally they came.

'Dad's going to be an invalid for life.'

Nicola's shock and disbelief was plain to see.

'No!'

'Yes. He fell, cracked his skull.'

As she spoke the words once more the pictures were in Donna's mind's eye, and again she was fighting the tears. After a while she managed to win the battle and she continued.

'But the worst of it was they found why he fell.'

Nicola waited patiently to hear what was coming next without making any comment.

'They've found his kidneys are dead, Nicola.'

'No!'

'Yes. Both of them. He's on one of those dialysis machines to keep him alive, and he'll have to be on it for the rest of his life.'

Nicola was shocked beyond belief. All who knew Jim knew what a smashing bloke he was, and Nicola was no exception.

'Oh no!'

A little anger had flown into Donna at the memory of what was coming next and it helped to fend off the tears for a while.

'The doctor seemed so unconcerned – it seemed he could condemn somebody to be an invalid for life without giving it a second thought.'

Nicola desperately looked for some glimmer of hope.

'Couldn't they give him a transplant? You read about it all the time.'

Donna was now firmly back in control as they reached that common ground.

'That's the first thing I said to the doctor. He just didn't even want to talk about it.'

Nicola thought about it. And then realised she may just have the answer.

'I suppose because as there's less and less donors these days – didn't want to get your hopes up too high."

Donna was suddenly all ears.

'How do you mean?'

Nicola decided that even if it wasn't right it would cheer Donna up to hear the thought so she let her have it. 'Well, let's say they were looking for a donor; and can't find one; then you'd really freak. But if they were doing it secretly so as not to raise your hopes ... '

Donna sat up at the thought. For the first time a glimmer of hope had appeared on the black horizon.

'Nicola! You could be right. He's a rare blood group, be a job finding someone who matches it. But if you were right and they are at least trying! Oh, Nicola, that would be wonderful!'

And with that she gave Nicola a hug, and Nicola was pleased she had given Donna room to dream.

When school was through for the day, Spuggie decided to go and see how Fraser was getting on. She arrived at the base of the flat and looked up at its towering ugliness. She wasn't pleased to be there, but she did think the least she could do was offer to help. So, much against her better wishes, she trudged up the stairs to face up to it.

Perhaps if she could have seen Fraser by then she may have felt differently.

He had managed to get the place spick and span from top to bottom and had now settled at the kitchen table to catch up with outstanding school work, the whole point of the off site day in the first place.

The sound of the doorbell breaking into his studies surprised him. He looked at the clock and realised it could be Spuggie. He crossed to open the door and found he had got it right, Spuggie looked him up and down and then grinned.

'Suits you.'

Fraser was a bit surprised.

'What?'

She chuckled and pointed, and he finally realised he was still wearing his mam's pinny. He took it off, asking the question as he hung it behind the door.

'So what brings you here?'

She crossed to sit at the kitchen table.

'Thought I'd come and help.'

Fraser also crossed to sit back at the table.

'It's done.'

'Why did you do it today, Fraser?'

He looked up but didn't reply.

'Why today?'

He finally decided to tell her.

'Mam's looking really good, Spuggie. Chances are she could be out of the hospital quite soon.'

Spuggie said what she had to say quite quietly, knowing it was a kind of betrayal.

'Would we have to come back here to live?'

'Yes. Of course.'

Fraser could see from her face that there was a sadness there. A sadness he could not understand.

'We can't go on living at the Gallaghers' forever, Spug. We're a family, You, me, Mam. We're a family.'

She hated herself for saying it, but she had to.

'I don't want to come back here, Fraser. Before, what it was like didn't matter, because we'd never known owt different. It didn't matter if there wasn't proper meal times, that we never had any clothes never mind clean clothes, didn't have to have baths, stuff like that, It didn't matter. But once you've seen what it should be like, what it's like for other kids, you want it too. And it's never going to be like that here, Fraser.'

Fraser had been dreaming all afternoon of just such a home, and he didn't want Spuggie smashing his dreams so quickly.

'It could be like that, Spuggie. It could be. We just didn't know how to help make it happen before. Now we do. Give it a chance.'

She was very sad to have to say it again, but it was the truth.

'I don't want to come back here, Fraser. Ever.'

She realised that there was not a lot that Fraser could say in the face of such an ultimatum, so she went for a change of subject. She dragged a pile of framed photographs that Fraser had collected earlier from various points in the flat and looked through them.

'What about these then?'

As she glanced at them she realised the common denominator.

'They're all of Dad?'

Fraser replied slightly defensively, as if expecting some protest from Spuggie.

'That's right. I'm hiding them away – don't want Mam to go upsetting herself by being reminded of him when she gets back.'

Spuggie continued to look through the photographs a little longer before saying it.

'You think he'll come back one day, Fraser?'

His reply came with such unexpected and sharp bitterness, that Spuggie looked up at him.

'Who knows? Who cares? Who needs dads? I'm "man of the house" now. He can go get stuffed.'

Spuggie smiled at hearing the lovely old northern expression, 'man of the house' and decided to wind Fraser up with it a bit.

'So, how does the "man of the house" feel about taking his little sister to the early pictures?'

Fraser was suitably shocked at such an outrageous and expensive thought.

'You've got to be kidding.'

Spuggie decided at least to give it a bit of effort now she had opened up the subject.

'Oh go on, Fraser – it's a great picture! And you've got money now you're working, and I'm skint.'

And then, to her amazement, he said yes!

The large room at Byker which had earned the nickname of the committee room, because of the number of conferences the gang had held there over the years would normally be fairly noisy, but tonight it was in an uproar, PJ having dropped his suggestion for earning the money for Gill's memorial into the conversational melting pot. Winston was the first one to make his voice heard above the general racket.

'What sort of a show are you suggesting we should do, PJ?'

PJ replied without any hesitation.

'The sort of show that people pay good money to see.'

Duncan as treasurer was less than enthusiastic; he felt this idea could cost rather than make them money.

'You said that before. Said we should do a magic show but that didn't come off, now, did it?'

PJ as ever managed to turn the battle and put Duncan on the defensive.

'I gave you my magic books; so what you grumbling about?'

And as usual succeeded with the ploy.

'I'm not grumbling, I'm asking.'

That PJ could happily handle.

'Magic was too narrow. We still do it, but we open it up a bit, give the show wider appeal.

On the edge of the group Kelly was perplexed.

'Like how?'

The question was one that PJ was waiting for.

'Variety – lots of different acts.'

And it was Debbie who then asked the obvious.

'But who we going to get to do them?'

Immediately a smile beamed from PJ now he was coming to the best bit.

'*We* are going to do them.'

There was then a reaction that showed the total disbelief they all had in the possibility that they might be able to do it. It was Tessa who made the sensible decision to find out more before condemning it out of hand like the rest seemed set on doing.

'What sort of thing have you in mind, PJ?' she asked.

And it then turned out that the project was wide open.

'Anything we can think of. Winston could do a dog act.'

Thinking of the dog that Winston had been trailing around lately it was no surprise that everyone laughed.

'I'd have to get it to teach me some tricks first.'

Kelly was surprisingly pleased at the thought, and decided to throw in some encouragement.

'You could do it, Winston – be great. I'd help. I could be your assistant.'

A voice from the back of the crowd called, 'What about you, PJ?'

PJ again had no hesitation.

'I'll borrow a unicycle – do an act on that.'

Everybody was amazed. They had no idea that PJ could do that. Debbie's question cleared the mystery.

'You can ride a unicycle!'

He had the grace to tell the truth.

'No – but I could learn.'

The chatter about the project continued to grow, and PJ could sense that warmth towards the idea was growing. It was Duncan who confirmed it.

'I could do one of the illusions out of the magic book.'

The remark Debbie then made cracked everybody up.

'Couldn't make our Jemma disappear, could you? For good.'

And Duncan's reply got an even bigger hoot.

'No – but I could saw her in half.'

There was a roar of approval at the thought but Debbie saw the snag.

'But then there'd be two of her!'

And the final ring of laughter was so loud, it could even be heard in Geoff's office.

Sitting in that office and hearing the distant laughter, Speedy began to wonder whether he had made the right decision to seek help from Geoff about his recent sleeping problem. The fact that Alison was sitting in on the discussion didn't exactly help. It was Geoff who finally broke the silence that had descended.

'If you won't tell me what the dreams are about, Speedy, how can I help?'

Speedy thought about it. How could he tell them he was going crazy with thoughts of Charlie. They were sure to laugh at the thought. He knew he couldn't do it.

'I don't know – just thought you might have some ideas that's all. I'm losing a lot of sleep.'

But Geoff, as was his way, kept digging away at it.

'I might have some brilliant ideas – but give me something to go on.'

The bang on the door, heralding the arrival of the gang came as a relief to all of them. Geoff called out gratefully:

'Come.'

And it was PJ who opened the door and popped his head in.

'Got a minute, Geoff? We're going to make a fortune for the memorial fund.'

'With you in a bit.'

PJ saw Speedy sitting there looking glum, realised he was probably on the carpet for being such a misery. As he closed the door Geoff was speaking.

'Have a think – see if you can come up with anything more for me to go on, Speedy. Maybe then I'll be able to help.'

And with that, quietly relieved to be out of it, Geoff stood and headed for the door.

As the door closed behind him Speedy realised that Alison was looking at him quite intently. Finally she spoke, gentle.

'Speedy . . . '

'Yes?'

A pause before she said it.

'Are you in love?'

Speedy was immensely relieved to hear the words said for him, without having the embarrassment of having to say them for himself. 'Yeh. I think – I am.'

In the committee room it had taken only minutes for them all to get their idea off their chests and let Geoff know what they had in mind, words falling from each of them like an overlapping waterfall. Finally as they ran out of steam and silence fell once more, PJ asked the question.

'So – what do you reckon, Geoff man? Are we on?'

The pause hung in the air as they waited with bated breath for Geoff's reply, as ever his face not giving a hint as to what the answer might be. When it came its brevity shocked them.

'No.'

It was PJ's voice that cut through the instant furore.

'But it's a great idea, Geoff man! Put Byker on the map.'

Geoff was ready for that one.

'Put Byker in court for taking money under false pretences more like.'

And all immediately were thinking how they could deny the possibility. Duncan and Winston were the first to pipe in.

'I'm going to saw Jemma in half.'

'I'll be doing a dog act.'

And soon all the voices were raised again as each in turn called out what they intended to do. Geoff finally called loud enough to break through all the chat.

'Hang on! Hang on! Hang on!'

And finally silence fell, and Geoff stated his proposition.

'This is as far as I'll go. You put the show together, audition it for me, and if it is any good at all, we'll advertise it and put it on . . . '

Instantly they cheered, and Geoff again had to raise his voice to be heard.

'But if it's duff – the deal's off.'

It was PJ who said it for all of them.

'Don't worry about that, Geoff – it'll be great.'

Which they all volubly agreed.

Alison and Speedy were strolling outside in the evening cool of the grounds. Alison saying what she had to say to a disbelieving Speedy.

'Just get it down on paper – whatever you're thinking – give you a chance to see it in black and white and stop it just going round in your head all the time.'

Speedy, who wasn't a fan of writing at the best of time, struggled to get her meaning.

'You mean a diary, like?'

She smiled, sensing his disbelief that such a simple idea could possibly work, but knowing from her own experience that it was the best therapy in the world for an aching heart.

'Whatever way it comes. It doesn't matter. Prose, poetry, whatever.'

For the first time Speedy laughed out loud.

'Poetry!'

But Alison wasn't the least offended, just went on to quietly explain it.

'Don't knock it, Speedy; sometimes things are too hard to face in the clear, and poetry's a way of walking round them without getting too near the fire and too badly burnt. The language of love since time began.'

And Speedy, seeing that she really meant it, started to consider it seriously for the first time.

Having sorted the gang out, Geoff was on his way back to the office when he saw Jemma, quietly sitting reading a book by herself. He was fascinated to see that she had cotton wool blobs sticking out of her ears. He crossed to where she was sitting and looked down at her. Finally realising she was being stared at, Jemma looked up at him as he spoke.

'What's going on?'

'What?'

Geoff repeated the remark, but this second time just mouthing it.

'I said, what's going on?'

Jemma was now perplexed at the total lack of any sound.

'I can't hear a thing, Geoff.'

In mime he indicated she should take the cotton wool out of her ears. Finally she did so.

'What is it, Geoff?'

'What's going on?'

'On?'

'Why the bunny rabbit impression with the great ball of cotton wool sticking out your earholes?'

Jemma thought about it, then decided there was no harm in telling him.

'We have a new kid in class – he's deaf, couple of the kids took the mickey . . . '

Geoff's reaction was immediate and serious.

'Not you, I hope.'

And Jemma's response was just as quick.

'No way – especially not after today.'

Geoff sat beside her before speaking.

'So what happened today?'

'Teacher gave us a project – the whole class has been hard of hearing for the day. Cotton wool in our ears.'

'How was it?'

'At school it was rotten – really hard to keep track of what was going on. Here it's not so bad – '

At that the gang were noisily trooping down the stairs and past the point where Geoff and Jemma sat. Jemma pointed at them to explain her point.

'Shuts that lot out for a start.'

Geoff grinned at the thought, and decided she had got a point. Seeing Speedy and Alison coming in the front door, he stood, and after saying a quick goodbye to Jemma, headed in that direction.

He called as he approached them.

'Want to get back to it, Speedy?'

But Speedy's face was now wreathed in smiles.

'Naw – it's all right, Geoff, – I think Alison's cracked it. See you.'

And with that Speedy was going off happily towards the tea bar; Geoff looked at Alison questioningly. She smiled back at him but was not giving anything away. This was her and Speedy's secret. Geoff recognised the look, and made his remark without rancour.

'Suit yourself.'

Speedy, parched after all the serious business of chatting on about his problem, was set on getting a coffee. He turned the corner, and then was stopped dead in his tracks. There in front of him was the very seat of his problem. Charlie.

Not knowing what she was secretly putting him through every night, she greeted him as cheerily as ever.

'Hi, Speedy.'

Speedy felt himself blush, not knowing what he could possibly say, and then before he could stop himself, his mouth was saying it for him.

'I dreamt of you last night . . . '

Charlie was quite pleased. Bit of a compliment to have someone dream of you even if it was only Speedy.

'Did you?'

Again Speedy didn't want to say it. But his mouth was now totally out of control of his brain and he said it.

The punchline of PJ's gag.

'No – you wouldn't let me.'

He watched fascinated as Charlie's beautiful face first went white, then started to flush red, and finally boil to a furious anger. As if in slow motion, he saw her hand start to lift and palm open head for his cheek, and made no effort to avoid the flat-handed blow that was coming. The sharp slap as it landed echoed through the room and brought him to his senses once more, and he stood there silently as she turned her back on him and walked away.

Speedy glanced around and saw that the whole gang were there watching in the distance, staring at him not believing the instant drama that had been played out.

Speedy decided he had had enough of Byker for one night, if not for good, and still being watched by the silent throng he headed for the door and went off into the growing gloom.

Donna sat silently beside Lisa as they made the long drive from the pub to the hospital for evening visiting, thinking over the endless day that had passed.

She had called the hospital on the hour every hour to enquire how Jim was, knowing that if he had shown any sign of waking she would have immediately dashed there to be at his side. But the answer each time was exactly the same – no change. He was stable though still unconscious. Donna couldn't recall the exact moment in the day when she had realised what she must do to save Jim from a lifetime of incapacitation, but when the thought had finally come to her she had felt a warm glow of joy. Here was the chance for her to perform a totally selfless act for once. An act that would finally let Jim know exactly how much she cared for him. But now, before they went inside the hospital, she was going to have to break the news to Lisa of what her intentions were, and if possible get Lisa on her side. She didn't quite know why that was important, but somehow realised that it would be.

The car pulled into the hospital car park and Lisa parked it deftly, switched the engine off, and was all set to get out when she noticed that Donna wasn't making any move to join her, but simply sitting there staring out of the front window, into the gloom.

'What is it, Donna?'

Donna finally turned to look at her, and there was a sparkle in her eyes that Lisa had never seen there before. Lisa waited for Donna to speak and when she did the words came with a strange fervour.

'I think I should tell you before we go in – I've made my mind up . . . '

She stopped, as if frightened to put it into words. Lisa tried to help with another question.

'You've made your mind up about what, Donna.'

Donna looked back through the window and into the night. Then having found the words, dropped the bombshell.

'I'm going to offer to donate one of my kidneys to Dad.'

Lisa sat back heavily in her seat. A long, long pause before she made the comment that was the last thing in the world that Donna was expecting to hear.

'Well, I'll give you this, Donna, you never miss a trick.'

Donna was totally thrown by the remark. 'Oh, aren't you brave.' 'Well done Donna.' Anything like that would have done, but Lisa's chosen comment, in the face of what Donna had just told her, made no sense at all.

'How do you mean?'

And Lisa's reply came like a slap across the face.

'Even at a time like this – when your dad should be the centre of attention; you'll manage to swing the spotlight back on you.' Donna felt her face flush with anger at the sheer enormity of what Lisa was suggesting. How could she possibly even think that Donna would be doing anything so crass as to be seeking glory at a time like this.

Finally Donna got enough control of her emotions to quietly ask the question.

'How do you make that out?'

And Lisa spelt it out for her.

'You make an offer you know they can't accept – and then you get all the glory without any of the pain.'

Donna was fighting tears, set on not letting Lisa know how deeply she had managed to cut her, so it was a long time before she could bring herself to say the words. But when they came they carried the weight of a vow.

'I'll prove you wrong in the end, but one thing's for sure; I'll never forgive you for that; ever.'

And with that she was out of the car, slamming the door behind her, and heading for the doors of the hospital. She didn't want Lisa to see that, having finally lost the fight with her emotions, she was now in floods of tears.

Spuggie's eyes were searching the late rush hour traffic looking for Fraser and his bike. She wasn't sure which direction he'd be coming from as the cinema complex they were going to, recently built by some entrepreneur who reckoned that there was soon going to be big money in the flicks once more, was not one that they had used before. But, as it was the only cinema in Newcastle that was screening the film Spuggie was so desperate to see, and the chances were, she thought to herself grimly, that if Fraser didn't put in an appearance soon, she would have to go on being desperate. Already the crowd had started pouring in for the next performance and still no sign of him. She jigged from foot to foot in her anxiety and said it softly to herself as if helping him along. 'Come on Fraser! Get a move on.'

Fraser, approaching through the heavy traffic on far side of the road, saw her before she saw him, and he recognised from the little jig of impatience she was doing on the spot, that she was going to give him a mouthful as soon as he arrived.

There was an underpass at the corner ahead. Joining the opposite sides of the street, and letting people get under the traffic from the nearby underground station to the busy cinema complex without risk.

Seeing it, Fraser smiled as the thought struck him. He could either cross to the other side of the road through the busy traffic, and get an earful of Spuggie while he locked his bicycle up to the railings over there. Or he could lock it up to the railings on this side of the road, then cross to the other through the underpass, and put the nagging off by a few minutes.

'Got to be the answer,' he thought to himself.

He soon arrived at the corner, and then got off and started chaining the bike to a handy railing.

'Fraser, where you been? We're going to be late! They're going in! Hurry it up!!'

Fraser smiled as he waved to her where she stood furious at the kerb opposite, he found it quite funny that with a roaring flood of four lane traffic flow she could still manage to make herself heard above the racket. He reckoned in another life she had probably been a town crier or something.

'Come on, Fraser! We'll miss the beginning.' Once more the call came and once more he waved at her to let her know he'd got the message. Having made sure the bike was safely tied up he headed for the underpass. Fraser didn't particularly like underpasses. They were always somehow a bit seedy and dirty, and the one he was going into proved his point. It was badly lit and graffiti covered every wall. As he went down the ten steps that led to the tunnel itself he noticed that the convex mirror, high on the wall that should have showed if anyone was waiting round the corner intent on mugging the unsuspecting traveller, had been sprayed over with a dun-coloured paint to remove any reflective qualities it might have had in earlier days. Not that he was worried that he might get mugged. There were loads of people using it, and it was highly unlikely at this time of day, but it was just the thought of somebody actually doing the mindless vandalism that got to him.

Fraser had found that when he did have to use any underpass, he always played a quick little game with himself before he turned the corner, 'Guess the beggar'. He would decide whether it was going to be some old man with his cap on the floor blowing tunelessly into a broken mouth organ, beggar boy with plaque, 'Homeless and hungry' scrawled on it, or somebody playing the bongos, or whatever. This time he guessed it would be a girl playing a guitar. As he reached the bottom of the stairs and turned into the tunnel the stench of stale urine struck and he gagged against its acrid smell. Ahead he saw that he'd got the beggar game wrong yet again. It was a ragged old woman who had the pitch. The black polythene bags at her feet obviously carrying her worldly possessions. As she stood there, she was intoning the same monotonous cry over and over again.

'Got any spare change, mister? Got any spare change, mister?' in a self-pitying whine.

But Fraser didn't feel any pity. He just felt a sense of outrage that anybody should let themselves fall so low as to beg in such a disgraceful manner. And then he went on to think of what her family must be like to let this old woman end up in an underpass begging for coins. The flood of people passing her, heading for the cinema where they would spend pounds were ignoring her pleas for pence, none responded to her request for change but simply hurried past without looking at her. 'Quite rightly too,' Fraser thought to himself.

If she wasn't encouraged maybe she would finally give up and get herself together. Get a wash perhaps. He could see even at this distance that her face was caked with dirt, and obviously hadn't seen water for days. Without knowing it, Fraser's lips had formed into a tight, sneering, unforgiving line. She was repugnant. He was by now close enough to see that she was dressed in a ragged black coat tied with pins at the throat and waist. She was simply disgusting.

As he passed her he was not afraid to look at her and let her see from his face how she appalled him. She pleaded directly at him as he passed.

'Got any spare change, mister? Got any spare change, mister?'

Fraser gave her a dismissive glance.

And then he stopped dead in his tracks, and felt as though he had been kicked in the heart by a horse.

He knew this woman. Had cuddled to her in his childhood. She was the one he had run to for comfort when he had been hurt.

It was his mother.

His mind reeled with the unbelievable shock of it. It couldn't be her, she was in hospital, slowly getting better. But there was no mistaking her, even though her face was filthy, there was no mistake. It was his mother.

'Got any spare change, mister? Got any spare change, mister?'

He took her shoulders, trying to make her look at him.

'Mam. It's me, Fraser. What are you doing here, Mam?'

Her watery eyes, blank and empty pools, looked but didn't

see him, didn't recognise him. She continued to plead even though he held her.

'Got any spare change, mister? Got any spare change, mister?'

He let her go. And then another shock. The voice screamed at him from the far end of the tunnel.

'Fraser!! What you doing! We're going to be late.'

It was Spuggie. Whatever happened he knew he must not let Spuggie see her mam in this condition.

'Wait there! I'm coming!!'

He quickly dipped his hand in his pocket and pulled out all the spare change he had, a few pounds' worth, slipping it into his mother's hand and curling her fingers round it. For the first time she changed her phrase, but still spoke zombie-fashion.

'Thank you, sir – you're very kind.'

'Wait here, Mam! I'll be back in a minute! Wait here right?!'

'Fraser, what you talking to that woman for!' Spuggie had started walking down the tunnel towards him as she had shouted. He almost screamed at her.

'Wait there! I'm coming!!'

And he turned to make one last plea to his mother.

'Don't move. I'll be right back.'

And then he was running to where Spuggie waited as the pleading started once more in the tunnel behind him.

'Got any spare change, mister? Got any spare change, mister? Got any spare change, mister? . . . ' distancing as they went.

Spuggie couldn't work out what was going on. As they had headed up the underpass stairs and then onwards towards the cinema, Fraser had cut her off as she tried to find out.

'So what was that all about?'

'Nothing.'

She noticed that Fraser was really pale and a bit shaky. *That's what comes from talking to bag ladies*, she thought to herself, and decided to give him a few facts of life.

'Don't want to go giving your money away to that sort – they'll only use it to get booze.'

He swung round to face her, really angry.

'Just shut it, Spuggie, okay! Okay?!'

Not a lot she could say to that, but she managed to find one sulky retort.

'Your money.'

When they arrived at the kiosk Fraser bought two tickets then gave her one.

'You go in – shan't be a minute.'

Spuggie was yet again bemused.

'Where you going? You'll miss the start.'

But Fraser was heading back towards the underpass stairs as he called the remark over his shoulder.

'You can tell me what happens.'

And Spuggie watched him going down the steps two at a time, then shrugged and went in.

Fraser leapt down the last three stairs, stumbled and almost fell in his haste to get back to his mam. He didn't know what he'd do when he got there, but he decided that he'd think of something. Maybe get her back to the hospital, or take her to the Gallaghers', to get her cleaned up. He'd think of something, he decided. At the entrance to the tunnel, one glance revealed that the worst thing that could possibly happen had happened. She had gone. Again he felt the kick in the heart that drove the word from his lips before he could stop it.

'No!!'

And then once more Fraser was racing for the other side of the underpass as quickly as his legs could take him. He knew she couldn't have got far, not carrying three big black bags she couldn't, might even now be walking up the stairs on the other side, so he ran as he had never run before. He collided with a man coming round the corner, who hadn't been able to see him hurtling along without aid of the mirror that had been painted over.

The man shouted at Fraser as they both fell in a tangle.

'Idiot! Why don't you watch where you're going!'

But Fraser wasn't interested in hanging about having arguments with strangers, so he leapt to his feet and ran on.

Up the stairs two at a time and then he was back on the same side of the road as his bicycle, anxiously looking around.

His mother was nowhere to be seen.

His mouth took over and screamed it even though there were people milling around.

'Mam!!! Mam – where are you?!!'

As he screamed it people started moving to one side to avoid having to go too near him. And as he screamed once more at the top of his voice, people stared at him as if he was a madman.

'*Mam!!!*'

And then it was all too much.

Fraser stopped calling, and went and leaned against the railings where his bicycle was tied. Leaned, and then, unable to stop himself, burst into floods of tears, quietly saying to himself over and over again through his sobbing.

'Mam, I love you. I love you, Mam. Where are you?'

CHAPTER THREE

Speedy awoke early the next morning. If he'd turned over and closed his eyes he probably would have gone straight back to sleep again, but rather than take the risk of yet another nightmare, he'd got straight out of bed. Now he was sat wrapped in the duvet, in a chair by the window, and watched the dawn creep over the green playing field in front of the house, that doubled as the largest dog loo in Newcastle. He had a writing pad on his knee and a pencil in his hand but words weren't coming easily, as his mind kept going back to the surprise meeting he'd had the previous evening.

After his unexpected and disastrous run in with Charlie, he'd gone mooching off to the Metro Centre, without any great hopes of finding anybody to pass the time of day with, but it turned out he was luckier than expected.

In one of the cafés Haley, the second half of the duo that Charlie used to record with, was singing along to the playing of a young male pianist who was maybe fourteen years old. Tall, blonde and sickeningly good-looking, Speedy noted.

He went in and got a coffee from the morose Italian behind the counter, and then took a seat in one of the corners to listen. It was a great tune, but the words were a bit naff, 'buttercups' and 'daffodils' and other unlikely lines for pop market potential. As the number finished Haley spied him and came over to his table as the kid carried on playing the song in the background.

'Hi Speedy. Long time no see.'

Speedy had the standard reply ready.

'As the ship-wrecked sailor said.'

Uninvited she sat and joined him.

'So – how's Charlie?'

Speedy rubbed his cheek at the memory of their recent run in, and replied rather ruefully,

'Still not pulling any punches.'

Haley missed the innuendo and carried on with the cross examination.

'How come you're not at Byker tonight?'

He lied easily enough.

'Sometimes good to get a change. How about you – what you been getting up to?'

'Still singing with the group – nice lot of bookings.'

Speedy found that a bit strange.

'So how come you're singing here as well?'

She smiled.

'One of the guys heard Danny playing the other night – thought he might have a song or two so I came to check it out.'

'Must be good to be playing here.'

'His uncle owns the place.'

She pointed at misery behind the counter.

'Ah. So – any songs?'

Haley pulled a face that said it all.

'Not our style – besides which he hasn't exactly got a way with words.'

'Buttercups and daffodils?'

'Exactly. Now I go gently break the news. Come and meet him.'

Speedy reckoned he had nothing to lose so he went over with her, they arrived just as he finished playing. Haley did the introductions.

'Speedy meet Danny, Danny meet Speedy.'

'Hi,' said Speedy,

''Lo,' said Danny, and offered his hand for shaking.

Though it wasn't the most usual occurrence in this neck of the woods, Speedy shook it as he spoke.

'What was the tune you were playing – didn't recognise it?'

When Danny replied it wasn't as a brag, simply stating facts.

'One of mine.'

Speedy was impressed.

'Sounds great.'

Danny smiled to take the edge of his remark. 'You haven't read the book *How to make friends and influence people*, have you?'

Speedy smiled back at the thought.

Haley being Haley couldn't let it get too cosy. She directed her remark at Speedy but it was aimed at Danny:

'You're right, Speedy. Great tune – rotten lyrics.'

Speedy didn't miss the faint flush that immediately tinged Danny's cheeks at the slight. He tried to joke the moment away.

'So that's what passes for breaking the news gently these days, is it, Haley?'

But Speedy need not have worried, Danny could obviously handle his own verbals. His remark was also pointed at Speedy, but Haley was the target.

'Mind you – my songs usually sound better sung in tune, being honest.'

And Danny got a bull's-eye. Haley was immediately furious.

'Up yours, Dimmoro – I came here to do you a favour. The guys could have made you.'

Danny went for the kill.

'Same way as they've all made you?'

Haley abandoned the cut and thrust of gentle repartee, and replaced it with a mouthful of foul abuse as she grabbed her coat and bag and headed for the door, and exited still swearing at the top of her voice.

The door slamming closed behind her left silence sitting heavy in the room, as the few other patrons present watched Haley going off in a fury. Speedy broke it.

'Great to see she's finally got that temper of hers under control.'

Danny laughed.

'I think, to be fair, I should put the record straight.'

'How's that?'

'Well – Haley was right and I was wrong. She sings in tune – but as to the words I write – I'm the pits.'

They both laughed at the thought.

Speedy had stayed on to chat with Danny, finding him good and easy company. He'd only recently arrived in town and hadn't had time to meet many people yet, so he was as pleased to chat with Speedy, as Speedy was to chat with him.

They rabbited on about all sorts of things and Speedy finally found himself passing on the advice he'd received from Alison earlier in the evening.

'She said it's a great idea to write what you're thinking down; so I'm going to give it a whirl.'

And Danny dropped the thought into the conversation totally unexpectedly.

'So why not try writing it like a lyric.'

'A lyric?'

'Sure – why not? If you're going to be writing in any case – why not try it?'

Speedy asked the question that would have made his English teacher wince.

'So what's the difference between a lyric and a poem?'

And Danny came back with a great answer.

'About half a million quid if you get the right one.'

And that's how it was that Speedy, having agreed to give it a go, was sitting up at the crack of dawn with a pad and pencil on his knee. He had agreed to meet Danny after school to see if anything had materialised. As Speedy had said at the time, 'Look – I don't promise to come up with anything, mind.'

Danny's friendly reply had cheered him no end.

'Don't worry – you couldn't write anything worse than I do.'

In the bedroom Speedy chuckled at the thought that he wasn't writing anything, good or bad, and he decided he'd better buckle down to it. He'd just thought of a possible first line and was going to get it down on paper when he heard the front door of the Gallaghers' open and then close. He leaned to look downwards through the window to see who else could be underway so early and saw that it was Fraser plus bike. He thought the thought out loud.

'So where's Fraser off to at this time in the morning?'

But, as Fraser pedalled off, Speedy was soon back buried in his pad, and his very first effort at song-writing was finally underway. Aptly he wrote, 'I'm a lonely man.'

Fraser's mind was in a turmoil as he cycled away from the house. He hadn't slept all night. Every time he'd closed his eyes a picture of his mother, filthy, dressed in rags and begging, floated into his mind. And now he didn't really know where he was going but had to go somewhere just to get away from the constantly recurring memory. Without being aware of how he got there, he found himself back at the underpass where he'd seen his mam the night before. He chained his bike to the same railing, and went down the stairs into the tunnel's dark smelly interior, his heart racing. For the first time he didn't play the 'guess the beggar' game, simply hoping she might be there.

She wasn't.

Fraser slowly walked to the centre of the tunnel, the point where she had been standing the night before, and wondered if he could have dreamt it, whilst knowing in his heart of hearts that he hadn't.

'Oye!'

The cry that came from the far end of the tunnel didn't register at first. It came again louder.

'Oye you!! My patch!!'

And Fraser looked in that direction.

There was a boy sitting on the steps at the far end. Fraser couldn't read the cardboard notice at his side from where he was, but guessed rightly what it would say:

'Hungry and Homeless. Please help.'

Fraser started walking in that direction as he called back.

'You talking to me?'

'Yeh. My patch. You can't beg here.'

As Fraser approached he saw that the boy had a filthy flat cap on the floor at his feet with a few pence in it. As he arrived he saw that the kid was quite young, and had the ferrety face of someone who might have happily appeared as an urchin in *Oliver Twist*.

'I'm not begging – I'm looking for someone.'

'Like who?'

Fraser walked round telling the truth.

'A woman. About forty-five.'

'I prefer young ones meself.'

Fraser managed to contain his anger. The kid was not to know how upset he was.

'Me Mam. She's not well.'

'So why'd she be down here then?'

Fraser looked back along the tunnel, remembering.

'She was here last night. She was supposed to be in hospital – but she was here – begging for change . . . '

Footsteps were heard coming down the stairs. The boy dropped his head on his chest as he spoke.

'Hang on!'

The first two people down the stairs walked past Fraser and the boy ignoring them, the third, a middle-aged woman, threw a pound coin she had ready in her hand, into his cap. As they went Fraser was amazed to see that the boy removed the pound from the cap and put it into a side pocket that rattled with many other coins.

'Why do you do that?'

The boy was bemused.

'What?'

'Put the pound away.'

The boy smiled his crooked little smile and pointed at the few coins in the cap.

'Nothing sadder than an unsuccessful beggar boy who's obviously slept out all night.'

'And have you?'

'No. But here I am at the crack of dawn, and they don't know that, do they?'

A few more people were approaching from the other direction.

'Look, hope you don't mind me saying so, but I'm supposed to be sat here sad, silent and depressed, and you're ruining my trade. I've got to go off to school in an hour.'

Fraser was suitably staggered.

'You go to school looking like that?'

The boy pointed at the plastic bag he was leaning against.

'Naw. Got me uniform in the carrier.

'That's incredible!'

'I thought you were keen to find your mam? You're not going to find her here while you're gabbing on now, are you?'

'I'm on me way.'

As Fraser started walking off the boy called after him:

'Look – maybe she went straight back to the hospital. Came out, earned a few quid to buy whatever she's into, then popped in again.'

Fraser turned to look at him, but kept walking backwards as

the conversation continued. 'I'm going there next. Hope you're right. Look, if you see her would you give me a shout?'

'How do I manage that trick?'

'Know Byker Grove?'

'The youth club place?'

'That's the one. Ring me. Ask for Fraser.'

'Is there a reward like?'

Fraser stopped in his tracks. He couldn't believe that any kid could be so mercenary. He finally called back angrily:

'Haven't you got a mam or what?!'

There was a pause before the reply came.

'Naw – she's dead. Died last year. Why do you think I'm here?'

A long moment then Fraser said it.

'There's a reward.'

About the same time that Fraser set off without too much hope on his journey from subway to hospital, Debbie was on the landing at the Dobson home, banging on the bathroom door once more, and bawling at Jemma, who yet again had taken up residence behind the locked bathroom door.

'Jemma! Will you stop doing this! You don't own the bathroom you know! Jemma! Get a move on!'

The only consolation was that at least this time Jemma was getting the message.

'I'm being as quick as I can.'

In between bouts of banging, Debbie pondered the unfairness of life. Some people had hundreds of loos, or at least two, and there they were, three growing kids and three grown ups, with only one lav between the six of them, plus the fact that one of their number seemed intent on taking up living in there. She had another quick pummel before calling. 'I hope you're not messing about making yourself deaf again!'

The voice, baffled by the door, was still clear to hear.

'I'm not.'

And indeed Jemma was not making herself deaf; this morning it was to be a totally different project. She finished whooshing water on her face then turned to the towel rail without opening her eyes, then finding the towel she dried her face. Still not opening her eyes she dropped the towel, as she thought back to the rail, but missed, and it landed on the floor, then braille fashion she felt her way back to the sink. She knocked the soap dish and soap onto the floor in passing, then knelt down to find them. Coming back up again she gave her head a bang on the sink and cried out in pain. Then having put the dish back in its place she searched for the bathroom cabinet, found it, opened its door, and searched for her toothbrush.

Bottles of her dad's aftershave and Nicola's deodorant going flying and crashing into the sink in the process. Debbie's voice could be clearly heard as she bawled yet again.

'What's going on, Jemma? You're wrecking the place.'

'Nothing! Just cleaning my teeth.'

And indeed Jemma had by then found her toothbrush, and had run it under the cold tap to wet it before putting the toothpaste on it. The trouble was that the feel of a toothpaste tube was of course exactly the same feel as her dad's tube of shaving cream, and that was what Jemma had actually got hold of, and what she had put on her toothbrush. Jemma's 'Ugh!' of disgust as she started cleaning her teeth with it, could probably have been heard three streets away.

Meanwhile breakfast was underway at the Gallaghers', and was for once a somewhat more sedate affair than usual. Speedy was at the table with his writing pad to one side, and without looking he was feeding himself with cereal whilst continuing to write.

Lou, entering the room with yet more fresh washing ready for ironing, made her comment in passing.

'You're going to miss your mouth if you don't watch what you're doing, Speedy.'

Which just happened to be the perfect feed for Spuggie who had also just walked in from her room.

'You gotta be joking, Lou – mouth that size, he could get the spoon in sideways.'

But Speedy's disposition this morning was much too cheery to be thrown by a mere Spuggie one-liner.

'Spuggie don't pick – I'm in a great mood.'

And Spuggie, having more important things on her mind decided to let it go.

'Where's Fraser, Lou?'

'No idea – bathroom?'

Still without looking up from his pad Speedy gave the news.

'He left yonks ago.'

Lou was surprised, Fraser being great at making his good-byes known.

'Really?'

Whereas Spuggie just wanted more information.

'To go where?'

For the first time Speedy looked up at her.

'How should I know – am I your brother's keeper?'

Lou was suitably impressed at the misquote.

'That's good that, Speedy – you want to try your hand out with a bit of writing one of these days – could be good at it.'

Speedy moaned at the thought.

'That's what I'm trying to do, Lou! But everybody . . . '

He didn't get to finish his complaint. Whether Robert's frightened cry, or the crash of his fall out in the hallway came first, would be hard to decide, but whichever way round it was, it was loud enough to kill all conversation stone dead and set the three of them running to his assistance.

Robert was sprawled in a crumpled heap in the centre of the hallway, but was already desperately trying to get his weak legs back under him into a position that would make it possible for him to raise himself to his feet once more.

Speedy had dashed and grabbed one arm, and Spuggie the other, while Lou looped her arms under his back and they all quickly lifted him to his feet at the same moment that Robert's angry cry rang out.

'Leave me alone! I'm okay! I can sort myself out!'

But too late, he was back on his feet. Lou immediately let go, whereas Spuggie and Speedy where still hanging on worried in case he might go over again. Lou said it quietly.

'Let him go, Spug. You too, Speedy.'

They both finally did so and without a further word, Robert slowly and painfully walked the few yards back to his room, opened the door, and disappeared inside.

A moment's hesitation, and then Speedy followed him, a decision he was going to regret for a very long time indeed.

In the corridor having watched Robert and Speedy go, Spuggie spoke her thoughts to Lou in a worried whisper.

'He's not getting better, Lou, is he?'

Lou lied gently and hopefully.

'Too much of a rush that's all, pet. He'll get there in the end.'

And Spuggie then knew the truth. Robert would be an invalid for life.

In Robert's room, Speedy stood open-mouthed as he faced the verbal vitriol that was being poured on him by the man he had come to consider as his best friend, despite Charlie.

It had started simply enough, he'd just said, or tried to say, 'Look, Robert – if there's owt I can do like . . . '

And Robert's first remark had also been contained enough. His voice tinged with quiet desperation.

'Just go, would you?'

Speedy was a bit bemused by this.

'What?'

And then, it was as if he had touched a button, and the anger and frustration flooded from Robert in a stream of words, and Speedy was caught in the flood. He screamed it at the top of his voice.

'Go! Get out of here! Get off my back! Lose yourself! I don't want you hanging around me any more!! You make me sick! Your every look calls me a cripple! I don't want to see it any more! Get out! Get out!! Get out, Speedy and don't come back!!'

For a moment Speedy stood and faced him. He knew his face had drained of colour. That he would be white as a sheet, and twice as crumpled. He felt tears stinging behind his eyes and fought them. And then, realising there was nothing he could possibly say in the face of such a total rejection, he turned and left the room, closing the door quietly behind him.

He might not have felt quite so bad if he had seen what happened then.

Robert let himself fall face downwards on the bed, and biting the pillow so that no noise would be heard outside his room, he cried and cried and cried.

At the Dobsons' much to Debbie's relief the lock finally clicked, and the bathroom door began to open.

'And about time too . . . '

And seeing Jemma she stopped what she was about to say dead in its tracks.

Jemma still had her eyes closed tight and was coming forward through the doorway by touch. Her hand shot out and before Debbie could avoid it, it was feeling her face.

'Ger-off!'

But too late. Jemma her face wreathed with smiles said it gleefully.

'Morning, Debbie. I can tell it's you from your fat chops.'

And Debbie watched her, bemused, as she continued to make her way down the corridor towards the kitchen and breakfast, feeling the walls for guidance as she went.

Nicola sitting glumly at the table, took over the sight of Jemma from Debbie who disappeared into the bathroom to seek relief; a bit like a runner taking on the baton in a relay race.

She watched as Jemma quietly humming to herself, felt for markers to guide her to her usual seat. Arriving there, she sat and then started searching out all the items she would need for her breakfast, braille fashion. She checked her bowl was there in front of her, then searched around the table for the cereal packet, found it and put it handy to one side of her bowl.

Having seen enough Nicola asked the obvious.

'So what's this latest stupidity?'

Jemma's head cocked to one side as if to hear more clearly, she hadn't realised anyone was there.

'It's not stupid, it's important. Disability appreciation. Yesterday we were all deaf, today half of the class is blind, and the other half are their helpers.'

Jemma having checked that her bowl was still in front of her, reached for the cereal packet as Nicola spoke.

'You help each other?'

And as Nicola spoke, she half raised herself in her seat, and stretched over to quietly move Jemma's bowl to another position.

Once more Jemma cocked her head as if to hear more clearly.

'What was that!?'

Nicola's voice was awash with innocence.

'What was what?'

'Thought I heard something. You're hearing gets very acute apparently.'

Nicola was desperate to hide her desire to giggle, finally managed to control it and spoke in a straight voice.

'I've read that somewhere as well. Mind you, you probably haven't been blind long enough for it to take effect yet.'

Jemma replied as she poured the cereal, as she thought into her bowl, but in reality onto the tablecloth in front of her.

'You could be right.'

Without making a sound Nicola was just about rolling out of her seat with laughter. As Jemma reached for the milk, Nicola had to bite the back of her hand to stop herself from giving the game away, as Jemma happily chatted on.

'Me and Angel are blind today – and the shrimp is our helper . . . '

And as the milk finally poured, hit the table and splashed back onto Jemma's legs, Nicola could contain herself no more and roared with laughter as Jemma screamed, stood, and finally opened her eyes to see the mess in front of her.

'You pig, Nicola! You did that on purpose!' But it was no good. Her comment was unheard. Nicola was on the floor and hooting uproariously.

There was no laughter in the Bell household. Donna simply sat morosely at the breakfast table, and picked at the egg and bacon Lisa had fried for her, as she remembered the long night she'd spent sitting with Lisa at the side of her comatose dad.

She would have gone on sitting there all night but finally the Sister in charge of the ward, had suggested they go home and get a good night's sleep, adding a promise that she would call if Jim showed any signs of recovery. She hadn't called, and now Lisa was on the telephone to the hospital checking to make sure there had been no change, her voice a low background to Donna's thoughts.

'Yes . . . Okay, thank you. You'll call if there's any change? . . .

Right. That's good to know.' The call finished; Lisa put down the telephone and crossed to sit opposite Donna at the table.

'No change. Still unconscious – but they say not to worry, it's not that unusual.'

Donna and Lisa had hardly exchanged a word since Lisa's cruel remark of the night before, and Donna wasn't intent on being cheery in her presence.

'Great. Don't worry. Wake up, Daddy we've got a surprise for you, your kidneys are dead.' Lisa was stung into replying a little more strongly than she had intended.

'Stop it, Donna! Don't you think I'm under a strain too.'

'He's my dad!'

'He's my man!'

The silence fell and hung between them like a shroud. It was Lisa who finally broke it, hoping to be on safer ground.

'You going to school today?'

Sick of looking at the remaining half of congealing egg on her plate Donna pushed it away from her as she spoke.

'Be no point. Can't work while I'm feeling like this. I'm going to the hospital.'

'They say they'll call when there's any sign of movement.'

Donna finally looked up at her defiantly, daring her to take up the challenge.

'It's the doctor I want to see.'

And Lisa took it without hesitation.

'Don't go starting that foolishness again, Donna – okay?'

Donna felt herself flush at the word 'foolish'. Who did this woman think she was?

'Whether you think it's a foolishness or not is beside the point – it's exactly what I'm going to do!'

Lisa for once out of control bawled it.

'You'd need parental consent!'

'And would you give it?'

'I doubt whether I could; but if I could I certainly wouldn't – it's a stupidity.'

Stung beyond measure, Donna looked for the cruellest remark she could come up with, and having found it, went for the kill.

'Why? Like to see him heading for an early grave would you, Lisa?'

Pleased, she saw that she had absolutely stunned Lisa who sat back in her seat as if she had been physically slapped.

Donna gleefully drove home her advantage.

'How much is he worth dead, Lisa?! Checked his policies yet?!'

Lisa came forward on her seat, and Donna realised that she was fighting to restrain herself from hitting her.

Just do it, Donna thought. *Just you dare do it and I will give you a lesson you will never forget.*

But Lisa didn't do it. With an effort she got control of herself once more. And as she spoke it was both ice cold and threatening.

'I shouldn't have said that to you last night, about you trying to get the spotlight, and you shouldn't have said that just now. We're quits. But if you ever say anything like that again, I'll have your eyes out.'

Donna stared back at her equally cold, and totally unrepentant. And it was Lisa who looked away first.

Fraser had called into the hospital, went to the rehabilitation unit, and found that his mother's bed was empty, the blankets neatly folded on top of it, the pillows on top of them, all ready for the next patient.

The bed told the story, but he still couldn't stop himself from asking the question of the staff. Their reply had confirmed his fears. She had had a relapse. Gone out boozing with two other patients.

When they came back the worse for wear, and were torn off a strip by the nursing staff, she had pointed out that she wasn't a prisoner, and discharged herself forthwith. They had no idea where she had gone to. Fraser left the hospital in something of a daze. He found himself back at the flat without remembering the journey.

Entering he had again called out for her hopefully.

'Mam?'

But obviously she hadn't been there, the place was still spick and span from his efforts of the day before.

Now he sat slumped at the kitchen table, and didn't know what to do next. Couldn't think of who to share this thing with. His one dread was anybody discovering about his mam's vagrancy, who then might, whether accidentally or purposefully, let Spuggie know what was going on. And whatever happened he knew he had to save Spuggie from that. If he felt like this with the knowledge, what would a kid of her age feel?

As Fraser was pondering the problem, Geoff was on Byker roof laying out the equipment for the job in hand, namely patching up the leaking down-pipe. It wasn't going to be easy to reach the place where the crack in the piping was, he was going to have to tie himself off to a handy stanchion and lean far out over a buttress to get to it, and he'd also need Fraser standing by to hang on to his legs just in case. Geoff also had his eye on the weather; there was no way the job could be tackled if it rained. At the moment it was fine but the storm clouds were gathering to the north of Newcastle and the wind was blowing them Byker way.

Alison was arriving and parking her car. Geoff looked over the parapet but he wasn't looking in her direction, he was looking towards the entrance to the club, and then he looked at his watch and shook his head disbelieving.

If there was need of proof that occasionally thoughts can be transferred over great distance, what happened then would have confirmed it. As Geoff looked at his watch, Fraser shook himself out of his torpor and looked at the kitchen clock. Eight thirty-five. A fractional pause as he tried to remember why the time was so important, then he had it. He couldn't stop himself but say it out loud 'Oh no!' as he remembered his promise to Geoff to be at Byker at eight-thirty on the dot. A good twenty-five minute cycle away, and already he was five minutes late. As he leapt up and headed for the door, Geoff was going down the stairs and heading for the tea bar at Byker with a face creased with an angry frown.

By the time he got there Alison was all ready to pour boiling water on the three mugs she had lined up on the counter.

'Just making coffee.'

'Make it two not three.'

Alison looked at him surprised.

'I thought you said Fraser was going to be in early sorting the roof with you?'

'I did; he was; he didn't: we aren't.'

In spite of his ire Geoff was quite pleased with the neat reply he'd found.

Then he remembered the problem.

'In about ten minutes it's going to be pouring, and we're going to have an even bigger damp patch upstairs.'

The more he thought about it the angrier he was getting.

'I've a mind to bullet him forthwith.'

Alison was not used to seeing Geoff quite so angry and tried to jolly him out of it.

'Hey come on, Geoff – not the end of the world.'

But he was not to be jollied.

'No. But a major repair bill could be the end of Byker, and wet rot doesn't hang about setting in! Beside which – a promise is a promise. I didn't exactly twist his arm to offer to help.'

And Alison, realising he was not to be placated, made coffee for the two of them.

As they sipped silent at their mugs, and thought their thoughts, once more a tidal wave of kids rippled over Newcastle heading for the battlefield called school, waving at each other as they went.

PJ had taken a different route than the usual, one that would land him up outside Gill's old workplace, where he hoped to get a favour done by one of the apprentices.

He was standing at the gate waiting, with a wreck of a bicycle leaning against the mesh fence beside him. It had been a racing bicycle at one point, but racing bikes that have had their back halves rolled over by an articulated truck don't ride too good any more.

PJ had found it on a skip the night before, and reckoned it was perfect for his purpose. He finally caught sight of a young bloke in a boiler-suit and flat cap, who was the one he was hoping to see and called to him.

'Hey mate!'

The lad, who was only about a year older than PJ, pulled away from the two older men he was walking along with and headed in PJ's direction.

'Yeh?'

'Didn't you used to work with Gill?'

'Yeh.'

'We're doing a benefit – get him a memorial.'

'And?'

PJ decided this one wasn't exactly the greatest conversationalist in the world.

'I need the help of a trainee fitter.'

'For what?'

Two words! thought PJ this is getting better. He pointed at what was left of the bike leaning against the railings.

'I wonder if you could turn that into a unicycle for me?'

The young man's face creased in disbelief.

'You a comedian or what?'

PJ gave the wreck of a bike another glance and then looked back to the lad.

'Shouldn't be that difficult. I was going to get a new one but they cost a fortune. I need one for me act, you see.'

The youth looked at the bike again, shook his head in amazement and then looked at PJ and suddenly, for the first time he smiled, as if he'd found an answer of some sort.

'You wouldn't be PJ by any chance, would you?'

PJ was a bit thrown.

'Yeh – how do you know that?'

'Never mind – I'll ask the boss if I can give it a go. Come round after school.'

Because of his sidetrack, PJ was a bit late getting to the place where he'd said he'd meet up with Speedy so they could walk in together, but Speedy didn't seem that fussed. He also didn't seem that interested when PJ wanted to know how the bloke at Gill's place could possibly have known his name from a simple little conversation. In fact all Speedy was interested in doing was waving the A4 pad he was carrying to emphasise any point he was making, and endlessly talking about his new-found career. After what seemed like hours of it, PJ had had enough. Speedy was just saying it yet again.

'I've got to tell you, PJ, it's great!'

When PJ cut through it. 'You *keep* telling me, Speedy! I submit, I submit! I agree it must be great.'

But Speedy was not to be put off by a bit of honest mockery.

'Honestly, man – it's amazing. Couldn't sleep so I started writing at the crack of dawn, and it just sort of poured out of me . . . '

PJ couldn't resist the jibe.

'Makes you sound like a kettle.'

And Speedy totally missed it.

'If I go on at this rate I'm going to have a bundle of words all ready to be put to music in no time!'

That gave PJ pause for thought, maybe there was a little opening for him in this new scheme.

'So who you going to find to put it to music?'

'Found him. Danny Dimmoro – Dimmoro's café in the Metro Centre.'

PJ joked again.

'He runs a café?'

And again Speedy missed it.

'No. His uncle owns it. Seeing him later, just hope he likes these.'

As he said that he once more indicated the A4 pad he carried.

Having missed out on the music side of it, PJ saw there could still be a possible opening.

'Well, I realise nothing may come of it, Speedy, but if by any chance you pull it off I know a great manager.'

'Who?'

'I'll give you three guesses, Speedy, and if the first guess isn't me – you can walk yourself to school.'

But Speedy wasn't listening any more. In the distance he had caught sight of a girl going into the newsagent's, and even from that distance he had no trouble recognising who it was. Charlie. He thrust his school bag and the writing pad at PJ.

'Hang on to these!'

And working on automatic pilot PJ took the offering. Then Speedy was off legging it for the shop.

'Where you off, Speedy?'

But too late, in seconds Speedy was out of earshot.

'PJ!'

PJ looked round to see who called, and saw that it was Duncan heading across the road to join him.

'Hi, Dunc. How goes it?'

Duncan's face was a touch forlorn.

'Not good. Any idea where I can get a cheap coffin?'

'Who you murdered?'

'Naw – it's the act. Need a coffin to saw Jemma in half.'

'Ask Geoff to make you one – the thought of making a coffin for you would probably cheer him up no end.'

Duncan was pleased with the advice.

'Good thinking – I'll do that.'

'I've got the unicycle organised – mate of Gill's.'

'Great – will you have it this evening?'

'Hope so. Got to go there after school see how he's getting on.'

'Right – see you then.'

As he set off PJ called:

'Where's Winston this morning?'

Duncan shouted back as he kept walking on. 'Him and Kelly were up to something. Don't know what, mind – thick as two thieves as usual.'

'Thick as two short planks more like.'

In the distance Duncan laughed at the thought.

'You could be right.'

But, in a local park, Winston and Kelly at that moment had just decided that it was the dog they had with them who had a screw loose. How could they possibly get an act together with a dog that just stood and smiled at them despite their best efforts.

'Sit!' shouted Winston for the umpteenth time, and the dog just stood there staring happily at them both. He tried it again a bit louder,

'Sit!!'

Still no movement. Kelly tried for an explanation.

'Perhaps it doesn't speak English.'

But Winston wasn't having that.

'Course it speaks English. It's an English dog. I mean if it was a poodle that would be different – I'd give the commands in French.'

Kelly was suitably perplexed.

'But you don't speak French.'

'Kelly! The chat is not helping! What do you suggest?'

She thought about it momentarily.

'Well – we could get him used to the command for what he's doing at any given time – and then take it from there.'

'You mean say "stand" when he's standing – and "sit" when he's sitting?'

'Yeh.'

'That's daft.'

'Wouldn't hurt to try.'

The logic of which Winston couldn't argue with.

'Okay – but I still say it's stupid, Stand!!'

And with that, still smiling, the dog sat down. Winston and Kelly exchanged a glance, then looked back to the dog. Winston was almost too tense to get the word out, but finally managed it.

'Sit.'

And dead on cue, still smiling, the dog stood.

Once more Kelly and Winston looked at each other, then both burst out laughing.

It was Winston who finally said it.

'You know what, Kelly – I think we may have the makings of an act.'

PJ sat on the low wall outside the shop that Speedy had disappeared into and waited none too patiently. He had always considered he had a comparatively high boredom threshold, but Speedy he decided was testing it to the full.

Occasional incidents lifted his spirits momentarily as he waited, Fraser racing past was one. PJ had called out, 'Hi, Fraser!' and got no response as Fraser was intent on pummelling the pedals at pace, and getting wherever he was going at the double, so PJ simply shouted to his retreating back, 'Bye, Fraser.'

Then Jemma and Angel wandered past with eyes closed tight

either side of Angel's minuscule brother, and the snatch of philosophical conversation drifted to his ears and provided the next bit of fun. It was Jemma who was doing the talking.

'So what is life all about, Angel? We get up, go to school, go home, go to bed, get up and go to school, what is life all about?'

They'd moved on a way by the time the reply came from Angel, but PJ managed to catch it.

'School holidays?'

And PJ smiled at the thought.

As it happened, if PJ hadn't been so bored he might not have flicked open Speedy's writing pad. But he was and he did, and Speedy was finally going to pay dearly for it. PJ immediately saw he had the chance of a wind-up of a lifetime, and who better to wind than Speedy . . .

Inside the shop it had taken Speedy a long time to pluck up the courage to talk to Charlie. She was one side of the shop's central shelving leafing through magazines, and appeared to be in no great hurry to make her choice, while Speedy stayed on the other side of the shelving and desperately tried to think of a conversational opening.

At that moment Charlie having made her choice, went to the counter and paid for it, then started to leave down the walkway that hid Speedy. Seeing him her face froze. Speedy didn't miss the look and decided he'd better start talking before she swept on out.

'Charlie – I just want to say I'm sorry about last night.'

Her reply was curt and unforgiving.

'I'm not.'

She started to walk past him heading for the exit.

'Wait! There's something I want to ask you!'

She paused, looking at him coolly.

'Like what?'

Speedy was totally caught out. What could he possibly ask her that would be of sufficient import to hold her interest. Then in a flash of adrenalin-driven genius he had it.

'I'm writing songs with someone.'

He thought her tone need not have been quite so incredulous.

'You!?'

'Yeah – me. Along with a bloke called Danny Dimmoro. I wondered if any of them came up to scratch, if you'd sing them for us?'

For the first time her face softened.

'Wait till you've got them and try me again – never know your luck.'

'Great! See you.'

Speedy decided to leave quickly while he was ahead of the game and on a winning streak, but her call stopped him at the doorway.

'Winston?!'

'Yeh?'

'How's Robert?'

It was as if she had thrown a cup of cold water over him. All morning he had been battling to keep the memory of Robert and his early morning remarks out of his mind, and to a large extent had succeeded, but now as she mentioned his name they came flooding back, and once more Speedy swelled with anger at the thought. He knew he should tell her that Robert wasn't too well, should tell her it might be nice if she called round there. But why should he? Robert could go get stuffed. And finally, such was the state of his mind, that the lie came glibly.

'Fine. Robert's fine. Never looked better.'

PJ saw Speedy coming from the shop and quickly folded and stuffed the piece of paper he'd nicked out of Speedy's pad, into his inside pocket.

At first he thought Speedy might have noticed but he was too full of his run in with Charlie to think of anything else.

Absolutely thrilled he gave PJ the news.

'Charlie said yes!'

'How good that is, Speedy, depends what she said "yes" to?'

But Speedy was too full of euphoria to see the possible implication of the remark.

'If they're any good – she's going to sing me and Danny's songs.'

PJ was a bit bemused at that.

'But you haven't written any yet? You're not seeing him till this afternoon?'

'Yeh, I know, but – what a terrific incentive.'

And with that Speedy grabbed his bag and pad, and PJ was pleased to see he was much too high in the clouds to even check their contents. The stage was safely set for a lot of laughs at Speedy's expense.

Charlie stood in the doorway of the shop and watched PJ and Speedy make their way to school. Then for a moment she thought of Robert. It had been days since she'd seen him, maybe she should go round. Then she thought of what Speedy had said. He was fine. She decided she wasn't going to crawl. If he wanted her he knew where to find her. Anyway, he probably never even gave her a thought these days.

In that she was wrong. At that very moment Robert sat in his room at the Gallaghers' looking out to the greenery beyond his window, without seeing it. All he could see was Charlie. And wondered how he could break his news to her.

There was the briefest tap on his door and then the door opened and Lou was there, a cup of tea in her hand. She closed the door behind her and came into the room, gave him the cup of tea and sat on the bed beside him. There was a long pause before she spoke. And when she did it was gentle.

'Want to tell me?'

Robert looked back out of the window as if contemplating it. Then having found the words he turned back to face her.

'They tell me I'm not doing as well as I should be. Somewhere there's an additional problem they can't quite put their finger on.'

He left a gap that Lou could have filled with a question, but instead she just waited for him to continue. Finally he did.

'They don't know whether it's mental or physical, but what they do know as far as they're concerned, it's the end of the line.'

To Lou her charges always became as dear as her children, and she sensed the hurt that Robert was bravely trying to hide. She put her arm around his shoulder and gave a friendly squeeze before asking the question.

'And?'

'I've got to leave here, Lou.'

'How soon.'

'They've applied for a long term stay for me, specialist unit down south – as soon as it's agreed – I go.'

Lou took her arm from his shoulders, and rested her hands together on her lap. It was time for her little boy to be allowed to be a man. Only one other thing had to be cleared up.

'And Charlie?'

Robert had thought of nothing else since he had received the news. It cut him to the core to think he would have to lose the person he loved to extinction. And in the face of such a monumental ache there was only one possible course of action. Pretend it didn't matter. The remark he finally made was said with an incredible defeated bitterness.

'Charlie's *yesterday*, Lou. The sooner I come to terms with that the better for both of us.'

CHAPTER FOUR

When Fraser finally arrived at Byker Grove, made even later than expected by a snapped main chain link *en route*, the first drops of rain were finally falling. But the blackness of the sky was no match for the blackness of Geoff's face as he stood in the front porch awaiting Fraser's arrival. Fraser's prepared apology was cut off mid-stream.

'Sorry, Geoff! Didn't mean to be late.'

'Well you are. Too late! We could have had it done by now – but we can't work in this.'

Fraser considered the weather was no great problem.

'I don't mind getting a bit wet.'

'We're not talking wet! We're talking dangerous! What the 'eck happened to you anyway!?'

In the normal course of events Fraser might have been tempted to tell the truth, Geoff was always a good listener, and knew how to keep his mouth shut. But in the face of his anger Fraser decided against it and went for the easy lie instead.

'Slept in – sorry.'

Geoff's sarcastic streak was on good form.

'Great, Fraser. When Byker finally caves in through rot – I'll make a big sign out of the bits saying "This happened 'cos Fraser wanted a bit more kip."'

With that Geoff turned and stormed inside leaving Fraser standing there feeling like a slightly soaked idiot.

Alison made him a cup of coffee while he dried his hair off, and then she suggested the job that might placate Geoff to some degree. The tea room door was catching on the bottom and she suggested Fraser got it off and took a sliver off its base.

Fraser agreed, put on a carpenter's brown apron, and got on with it.

If he'd known what a pig the job was going to turn out to be he mightn't have been so keen to accept. The screws were rusted solid and it took the best part of the morning to get them freed and out. The good news was that Geoff did mellow a bit as the morning progressed, passing through the tea bar at one point he stopped to chat.

'How's it going?'

'Bit of a pig to get the screws out, but only two to go, so should be off any time now I reckon.'

'Right. I'm going to sort the gear out up top. It's starting to look a bit brighter – with a bit a luck we'll get a crack at it before too long.'

'Great. Look forward to it.'

Little did they both know that at that moment an incident was taking place that would get in the way of the down-pipe repair yet again. During lunch break the beggar boy from the underpass, whose name it turned out was Lee, always did another half hour's begging. He got there changing as he went, a sort of reverse Superman deal. He went from neat schoolboy to ragged urchin in a flash, getting the change of clothes out of his carrier bag, along with his greasy flat cap, and cardboard notice, and then putting his school gear in the bag and out of sight. This transformation scene was played out as he walked the last hundred metres past the cinema, to the stairs that led down to the tunnel.

Arriving he realised he had competition for once. He could hear an old woman calling as he approached.

'Any spare change, mister? Any spare change, mister? Any spare change, mister?'

Running down the stairs he saw her standing at the centre of the tunnel bawling her monotonous refrain. He realised that chances were she could be the mother of the kid he'd spoken to that morning, so he went straight to question her.

'Have you got a son called Fraser?'

'Any spare change, mister? Any spare change?'

'He was here looking for you this morning.'

' . . . Any spare change, mister? Any spare change, mister? Any spare change, mister? . . . '

Lee realised he was getting nowhere and getting angry. Time was passing and he wasn't doing any business, nor could he while she was still here. First rule, one beggar, one patch. He tried to explain it to her.

'This is my patch you understand? You can't beg here – not at lunch time.'

He obviously wasn't getting through.

' . . . Any spare change, mister? . . . '

Lee made his mind up.

'Right! Soon get you sorted out lady.'

The tea room door was just hanging on by the last screw, and had bent over at a crazy angle as the telephone started to ring down the corridor.

Fraser was just trying to rest the door's weight by the wall as Alison called from the office:

'Phone call, Fraser.'

Fraser was a bit thrown. Couldn't think who on earth could be telephoning him here. Only way to find out he decided. Finally managing to wedge the door upright, he went off to take the call.

'Who is it?' he said to Alison as he arrived in the office.

'Young boy. Wouldn't say.'

Lee jumped from leg to leg in the telephone kiosk in the foyer of the cinema, impatient. Finally Fraser came on and recognised his voice.

'Yeh, it's me. Look not only is your old woman back down in the tunnel, but she's ruining my lunch time session, right? You can't have two people working the same patch, Fraser – it's useless, come and get her out of there . . . How can I keep an eye on her? I'm supposed to be a poor little beggar boy sat looking glum.'

Alison without meaning to was listening to the one-sided conversation from Fraser's point of view, and found it hard to fathom what was going on.

'Just do it! Watch her till I get there. I'll be as quick as I can . . Okay! Okay! I'll double the reward!'

At that Fraser slammed the phone down.

'So what was all that about, Fraser?'

But Fraser was on the move.

'No time to explain.'

He slipped out of the carpenter's apron and dropped it on the floor.

'Apologise to Geoff for me, would you, Alison – something's come up.'

'But I thought you had to get the guttering fixed before . . .'

But it was too late, Fraser was heading for the front door at a gallop.

On the roof Geoff was well pleased. Just like in the song, the dark clouds had drifted on, and it was now blue skies all the way. He and Fraser would have a good two hours of fine weather to get on top of the job.

He was just off to call Fraser and tell him to come up, when he glanced over the parapet, and to his amazement saw him pedalling off from the front of the building. He bawled at the top of his voice.

'Fraser! Fraser!! We can do it now!! You hear me, Fraser? We can do it!!'

And even though he heard the call, Fraser kept right on going.

Now there was definitely money in it, Lee was keen to get back and keep his eye on Fraser's mother. He left the cinema and walked the short distance to the tunnel and headed down the stairs taking them two at a time, but having gone into the tunnel he did a quick about-turn and walked straight out again. A double helping of the law was talking to the lady and obviously telling her to move on as is their way, and he could well do without mixing with their sort.

He watched as the old woman finally came out on the far side of the junction, then he did a quick and lethal run through the heavy lunch-time traffic, creating a cacophony of honking hooters as he went, so he could get to the same side and follow her.

Geoff having come back down stairs, stared momentarily at the door leaning at an angle. As if in response to his stare, the door slowly keeled over and fell crashing onto the tea room floor, wrenching its last screw out in the process. Having watched it settle he made his way to the office where Alison was typing away at the correspondence.

He looked at her quizzically from the doorway.

'Well?'

She stopped typing and looked at him.

'Fraser? What's it all about? Thought it was a bit funny him being late. It's not like him. This confirms it. Something's afoot.'

Alison only had a momentary hesitation about telling Geoff of the conversation she had overheard. If there was trouble best he was forewarned.

'On the phone he said "Follow her and the reward is doubled – I'll be there as quick as I can."'

Geoff thought about it, and in moment had the answer.

'Spuggie's done a bunk again.'

Alison also gave it just a moment's thought before she agreed.

'You could be right at that.'

In Dimmoro's café in the Metro Centre, Donna sat quietly sipping her coffee and thinking her thoughts. She'd been waiting for Nicola for nearly half an hour but for once wasn't irritated. She felt weary deep inside. Her project was proving harder to pull off than she had anticipated.

Nicola finally arrived in a flurry of hurry, and dumped her bags to one side before slumping beside Donna breathless at the table.

'Sorry I'm late – lesson went on a bit.'

'That's okay.'

Nicola who was expecting fireworks was suitably relieved.

'What'd the doctor say?'

Donna finished the last of her coffee, and called to the middle-aged misery behind the bar for two more cups before answering.

'He didn't. Wasn't there – but I talked to a nurse. Not going to be easy. I've got to get parental permission.'

When Donna had told Nicola that she was intending to offer to give one of her kidneys to her dad, Nicola had naturally presumed that Donna, being Donna, was just being overly dramatic yet again, but Donna had finally convinced her that she meant it, and Nicola found it an incredibly brave thing to consider doing.

'Can Lisa give permission?'

'Turns out not. But she wouldn't if she could – I asked her, and she said "no-way".'

Nicola thought about it.

'Probably knows your dad would freak if she even thought of it.'

'Or doesn't want Dad to live.'

The bitter remark caught Nicola off guard.

'What!?'

Donna spelled it out.

'Stands to reason, Dad dies, she cops a fortune in insurance.'

Nicola was aghast.

'Donna don't say that! Don't even think that! It's crazy!!'

'I've already said it.'

'Not to Lisa?'

Donna's silence was a confirmation that that was exactly what she had done.

'That's cruel, Donna! At a time like this that is cruel even by your standards!'

Donna was stung by Nicola's lack of sympathy.

'All I want to do is help me Dad! Stop him being an invalid for life! And she's standing in my way! Isn't that cruel?!'

'You've already said she can't give permission in any case!'

'But I didn't know that then, did I?!'

The silence hung heavy between them as the Italian brought the coffees over, and stood at the table waiting for payment. They both found fifty pence and passed it to him, and he went back behind his counter without a word. The door clicked open and Danny came in and crossed to join the man at the counter, and soon they were having a heated discussion ignored by Donna and Nicola.

It was Donna who finally broke the silence.

'I want you to do me favour.'

'What's that?'

'I want you to write a note from Mam – saying she's giving permission for me to donate a kidney.'

Nicola couldn't understand the need.

'Why don't you get Polly to write it herself?'

Donna's real mother was alive and well and living out of town somewhere with her latest boyfriend.

'Can't take the risk, she might refuse.'

Nicola shook her head in disbelief.

'If you think after what I've been through with the police, Donna Bell, I'm going to go forging notes and signatures you've got another think coming.'

There was a heartfelt plea in Donna's voice.

'Nicola!'

But Nicola was having none of it.

'No! And that's an end to it.'

And once more silence fell. This time the conversation of Danny and the man, which was getting a little heated, intruded.

'But why can't I play today, Uncle Paulo!'

Nicola could see them both from where she sat and was suitably impressed that not only could misery speak, and that he did so in a thick Italian accent, but that he was the uncle of the rather dishy young guy who she hadn't seen around before.

'Tell me that, Uncle Paulo! Why can't I play?'

'Because it is my saint's day – that's why!'

'Your saint will love hearing me play.'

'My saint will love having his ears rested.'

'But Paulo! Someone's coming to meet me here and make songs!'

'Tough, bambino! Not on my piano you make songs. Not today.'

Nicola watched delighted as the guy flushed with the frustration of his uncle's stone walling, felt herself smile, and Donna didn't miss the fact that she had lost her attention.

'What is it?'

Nicola came back from her musing a bit baffled.

'What's what?'

'The fascination?'

'There's just a gorgeous guy getting so over-heated at the counter that he's blushing, really funny.'

She smiled again, and the smile was instantly wiped as

Donna stood angrily and started gathering coat and bag together ready for the off.

'What is it, Donna? Where you off?'

Donna's voice quivered with contained fury.

'If you won't help and can't give me your attention for a few minutes without getting sidetracked, I'll go and find someone who can.'

'Hey! Cool down! Just 'cos I've reacted to a nice . . . '

She didn't get chance to finish the remark.

'My father is going to be a cripple for life and you've got sex on the brain! Who's cruel round here Nicola – you or me?!'

And with that she was storming for the door.

The noise of the instant row had been high enough to attract the attention of Danny and his uncle, and now they and Nicola watched as Donna barged out slamming the door behind her. Danny having finally got his eye on Nicola, smiled and called to her in his usual friendly fashion.

'So! There goes another great friendship!'

But Nicola ignored him, and grabbing her bags also headed for the exit and slammed out.

Paulo said it for his own benefit.

'With these Newcastle kids, soon I need a new door.'

But Danny heard it.

'When I've earned some money from my songs I'll buy you one.'

'No playing my piano today!'

And Danny knew the battle was lost.

Arriving at the underpass once again Fraser had gone straight down into its depths, and found it deserted.

Now he'd been hanging around the entrance for nearly ten minutes not knowing what to do next. Then he saw Lee approaching down the road at a trot. Fraser didn't bother to exchange any pleasantries when he finally arrived breathless, but got straight down to it.

'Well? Where is she?'

'Police moved her on.'

'Moved her on where?'

'They don't move you anywhere – they just move you on.'

Fraser was at a loss; what now? Lee saw it and smiled his crooked smile as he spoke.

'As a matter of interest, as there's money involved, I followed her.'

Fraser was all ears again.

'Where did she go?'

'Dosser land.'

'Cardboard City?'

'That's the one.'

Fraser's heart sank. Everybody knew Cardboard City. It was a vast area of wasteland and filth, now covered with acres of cardboard boxes, that nice people pretended not to notice when they were forced to pass in that direction.

'Whereabouts did she go in there?'

'No idea.'

'You mean you didn't follow her in?'

'You got to be kidding. I wanna keep me boots.'

Fraser saw he had a point. Everybody knew that if you weren't living there, it was a good place to keep well away from. If you were living there chances are you had nothing worth mugging for, apart from the odd crust of bread. Whereas if you weren't living there, everything was worth mugging you for, from warm coat to best boots.

'Will you come back and show me?'

Lee started to change back to his uniform as he spoke.

'Got to get back to school. Running late.'

Remembering their deal, he paused in his dressing and put his hand out.

'I reckon a fiver should cover it so far.'

Fraser was about to go into his pocket when he remembered he was skint

'I haven't got a bean on me.'

'Okay. I'll catch up with you later – but don't forget, you owe me.'

And with that Lee was off into the underpass and away.

Fraser only stood there a moment more, then he set off purposefully in the direction that Lee had come from.

He had decided to go visit Cardboard City.

School, the price that had to be paid for the very suspect and hard-to-fathom pleasures of childhood, was over for the day, and the tide turned as, weary, and on the whole not much the wiser, kids homed to tea and toast by the telly, or in the case of the Byker bunch to an evening of fun and frolic and who knows what adventuring.

Each had various ports of call along the way. For PJ it was back to the engineering works to see how Gill's mate had made out.

He had made out great. PJ sat on the work bench and watched as he put the final touches to a one wheel wonder.

'Great they give you the time to do it.'

'I told the governor what it was for, he was pleased to help.' Adding ruefully, 'At least he was pleased to have me help.' With that he straightened up satisfied and indicated PJ should take it.

'Right – there you go – one unicycle.'

PJ got off the bench and crossed to take hold of it tentatively. It was unarguably ace, but there was only one slight problem.

'Wonderful. Only one thing, you've forgotten the handle bars.'

The reply came back without hesitation.

'Unicycle's don't have handle bars.'

PJ pondered before saying it.

'But that's stupid – how do you keep from falling off?'

'PJ, I'm just the mechanic, you're the circus act, work it out for yourself.'

Ah well, PJ thought, having given his thanks and started the long wheel to Byker, Geoff would have the answer.

Whereas Speedy had gone straight to Dimmoro's café where Danny had broken the news over free cups of coffee, one of the perks of having a family business, that there was to be no piano-playing that day.

Speedy had wondered whether Misery could be made to change his mind, when Danny spelt it out.

'You don't know Uncle Paulo, Speedy. Once he says no – the no stays said, and the piano stays unplayed. So – I'm afraid we'll have to scrub round it for today.'

Speedy thought about it, a bit disappointed not to be able to get the new career underway, then he had it.

'It's not necessary to scrub round it.'

'How come?'

'Come on. Drink up and I'll take you.'

He didn't know why he hadn't thought of it before. There was an old piano at Byker that stood in one corner covered by a cloth. All he had to do was to convince Geoff they weren't just fooling around, and they were back in business.

As he drank up his coffee, Speedy realised he was looking forward to showing off his new found friend. He finished glugging it down.

'Ready?'

Danny did likewise.

'Sure.'

And they too were on their way.

Geoff was out front in the late afternoon sunshine, using an electric saw, to saw the small sliver of wood off the bottom of the tea room door, the job that Fraser had never got round to finishing. It was surprisingly hard going. In the days the door was made, doors were made to last. But Geoff knew if he just plodded on cart-horse fashion he'd get there in the end.

Being out in the open like that made Geoff an easy target for the early arrivals, one of the earliest of which was Duncan.

He stood silent and unannounced at Geoff's side and watched fascinated as the little blade jigged up and down through the wood. Geoff finally became aware of his presence, and that though it hadn't been spoken yet, Duncan obviously had a request. He switched the machine off before speaking.

'Yes, Duncan?'

'Wondering if you'd do me a favour?'

Geoff straightened to take the kink out of his back.

'Try me.'

'Wonder if you'd make me a little coffin?'

'Who you murdered?'

'Too late for that one, PJ got it in hours ago.'

'How about: "Well, you look quite well at the moment, shall we give it a few more days and see if you survive?"'

In spite of his next comment, Duncan's face didn't show a fraction of a smile.

'That's not bad. I'll laugh if it'll help getting you working on it.'

'Be quicker if you just told me what you wanted it for.'

'The variety show – I'm going to saw Jemma in half.'

'Ah.'

Then a thought struck Geoff.

'And does Jemma know this?'

Duncan shook his head.

'I haven't asked her yet – but she'll agree all right.'

'Ask her, she's inside.'

'Okay.'

And with that Duncan was on his way into the club. Geoff was about to continue with the job in hand when he saw PJ approaching purposeful, a strange object slung over his shoulder, with Winston and Kelly also bearing down on him not too far behind.

'Couldn't give me five minutes when you're through, could you, Geoff?'

Geoff's quizzical look asked the question for him.

'I just want you to show me how to ride me unicycle.'

And without waiting for a reply he too was heading for the front door, his place at Geoff's side being quickly taken by Winston and Kelly plus cheerfully smiling dog.

They just stood looking at him so he helpfully filled the gap.

'So what's it to be? Small coffin; borrow me buzz saw; unicycle lessons, or what?'

It was Winston who said it.

'We need a little podium.'

'Oh! A little podium,' Geoff said sarcastically. 'That makes a nice change.'

Kelly wasn't to be thrown, she indicated the size as she spoke. A metre across and half a metre high.

'It needs to be a round one; and about that high, so that the dog can be clearly seen performing.'

Geoff was suitably impressed.

'You got an act?'

Winston, pleased to be asked, gave the reply. 'Working at it. Watch . . . '

The dog was standing looking at them as if knowing he was centre stage.

'Sit!'

And without any hesitation at all the dog sat.

Winston and Kelly exchanged a glance. Then Winston tried again.

'Stand!'

And the dog stood.

They couldn't believe it.

Kelly tried it.

'Sit!'

The dog sat.

'Stand!'

The dog stood.

Totally unimpressed Geoff switched the saw on all ready to go back to work.

'Well – that should be worth a few quid of anyone's money. Stereophonic commands and instant obedience.'

Kelly leapt to their defence.

'It's not supposed to be like that!'

'Supposed to sit up and juggle, is he?'

Winston decided that Geoff was being totally unfair.

'Give us a chance, Geoff man, it's early days!'

And Geoff's reply was heartfelt.

'Aye – you're right there, Winston. I've never been this dazed this early for a long time.'

Duncan finally caught up with Jemma and Angel as they came out of the girls' loo. He asked the question little expecting the reaction he was going to get. Jemma was flabbergasted and let him know it.

'You've got to be joking!? Who gave you the idea I'd do owt as daft as let you chop me in half!?'

Totally thrown Duncan told her without thinking.

'Your Debbie.'

At which Jemma did her nut.

'Oh great! What a way to get your own back for not being able to get into the bathroom of a morning.'

Having not got the instant 'yes' he was expecting Duncan tried a little cajoling.

'Look there's no danger! I'll use Geoff's electric buzz saw so it sounds and looks really good, and put a bucket down to catch any splashes!'

He guessed from the horrified look on Jemma's face that he wasn't winning the argument, when her remark confirmed it.

'You've got to be crazy! There's no way I'm doing it, Duncan, so there!'

'I bet Houdini never had this much bother.'

Then out of the blue Angel came to the rescue.

'I'll do it Dunc!'

Duncan was suitably amazed.

'You will?!'

'Yeh!'

At which Jemma chipped in once more.

'Oh that's different then. If Angel thinks it's all right that's all right by me. I'll do it as well.'

'You can't do it as well! I only want one person.'

At which Angel chimed in again.

'I'll only do it if Jemma can do it as well.'

Defeated Duncan retreated.

The sliver of wood had just fallen off the door when Geoff realised that Duncan was back at his side.

'Well?'

'No problem. The only thing is, could you manage to make me a double-decker one, Geoff?'

Geoff's look said it all . . .

Fraser round about that point had just decided that he had passed one of the longest and most wasteful afternoons of his life. After leaving Lee it hadn't taken him too long to reach Cardboard City.

It was under a flyover, not too far from the city centre, and it spread for what seemed like miles, but was in fact less than an ugly acre. Arriving there he had been able to look down on its squalor from a bridge that crossed it. As he looked down on it for the first time, he remembered once seeing some pictures by an old artist called Hogarth, in a book in the school library.

What he remembered was that the pictures had been full of ugly people with twisted drunken faces, all bloated from booze, and ragged and filthy from lack of care, young and old alike had looked the same, squalid and degenerate. Being pictures he hadn't been able to hear what sort of noise those awful people were making, but he had imagined it.

The people in his view in the cesspit world below were making the same sort of noise he had imagined. Even though it was the middle of the day, he could hear drunken shouting, somewhere a woman screaming, young kids were running around wild chasing a frightened dog and throwing bricks at it, all of it the stuff of nightmares.

And somewhere down there was his mother. Finally the realisation came to Fraser that all these people belonged to somebody. They had sons, daughters, mothers, fathers. They were just people. People who had fallen on incredibly hard times. And anybody, including himself, could end up in this bottom of the barrel hell-hole called Cardboard City.

Having realised the truth of it, Fraser tried to pluck up the courage to go down and join them, but as he was making his way from the bridge down the embankment that led to the area, a fight had broken out beneath where he climbed, four men pummelling away at each other brutally, and he'd lost his nerve and gone back up again.

For the rest of the afternoon Fraser stood by his bike on the bridge, and hoped to see his mother perhaps coming out of the area again, but she hadn't. Now he decided it was time to give up his useless waiting, go home and get some food, but more importantly, first go back and face Geoff at Byker.

Having decided it, he got on his bicycle and pedalled off. He was not too far from the Grove when Spuggie crossed to where Geoff was sanding down the bottom of the door to ask her question.

'Where's Fraser, Geoff?'

He looked up and saw who spoke.

'Wouldn't I just like to know. But at a guess, looking for you.'

Spuggie was amazed.

'You're joking. It's him who's doing the disappearing.'

Geoff stopped his sanding and gave her his full attention.

'How come?'

'He went off first thing – not even a goodbye. And we're supposed to be off to see our Mam soon.'

Geoff saw that she was quietly worried, so decided to comfort.

'No doubt he'll turn up finally.'

As Spuggie headed on her way, Speedy and Danny arrived.

'Geoff. Meet Danny Dimmoro.'

Greetings were soon exchanged and Speedy was getting it off his chest.

'So you see, Geoff, we need a piano.'

'No problem, Speedy, as long as I don't have to make a new one, you're both welcome to it. And welcome to the club, Danny.'

'Thanks.'

As they moved off Geoff saw Fraser's arrival out of the corner of his eye, and settled back to the job in hand wondering how long it would be before Fraser came to get it off his chest. It was immediate, Fraser came across to stand in front of him almost defiantly.

'I suppose you want me to give me notice in?'

And Geoff saw without being told that Fraser had problems.

'I want you to give me some explanations.'

Fraser took a breath and was about to let it pour when Spuggie saw him standing there and ran to join battle with him calling as she came.

'What you playing at, Fraser?!'

Geoff felt she had a point, and said it as she arrived.

'Good question, Spug.'

Whereas Fraser was a bit surprised.

'What you mean playing?'

'Going off without saying a word.'

He knew there was no way he could tell her the truth.

'Something cropped up.'

'Are we going to see Mam or what?'

Fraser realised that was the one thing he had totally forgotten, him and Spuggie had arranged to go to the hospital that evening. He lied none too glibly and Geoff didn't miss the fact.

'We can't, Spuggie. Not today. Mam's, had a ... bit of a turn.'

Spuggie was instantly worried.

'Is she bad?'

And Fraser as quickly placated.

'No, no. Just not ready for visitors at the moment.'

Having had her mind settled she was ready for more entertaining company than a brother.

'That's all right then ... '

She set off for the front door again throwing her remark over her shoulder as she went.

' ... won't have to leave the Gallaghers' for a while longer.'

Fraser watched her go, and then Geoff's question broke through his thoughts.

'Is that what it's been about – your mam?'

'Yeh.'

'How bad?'

'So bad I can hardly bring myself to think about it, Geoff man, never mind talk about it.'

And Geoff was wise enough not to pry. His next remark declared the truce, and put the battle field behind them.

'Eight-thirty tomorrow?'

For the first time that day Fraser felt really happy.

'Great! Thanks, Geoff.'

PJ having seen Speedy getting himself organised at the piano gathered the gang in the committee room above and broke his news.

It was wind-up Speedy time.

Everybody was there. Duncan, Winston, Kelly plus dog, Debbie, relieved that Jemma and Angel weren't hanging around, but instead had gone to lean on the piano and irritate the new bloke that Speedy had brought along. And finally the comparative new girl Tessa.

When PJ showed them the piece of paper he had stolen out of Speedy's book that morning, and told them what the plan was, they whooped.

'So what we got to do is learn a line each, right, then we'll do it for him, show him what it sounds like.'

It was Tessa who asked the dumb question.

'Does Speedy know you've got it?'

But being newish PJ didn't tell her how dumb the question was, just explained.

'Course not, Tessa – wouldn't be a wind-up then, would it?'

Everybody laughed at the thought.

And at the very same moment Speedy, sitting on the double piano stool alongside Danny, was searching through his pad for the lost lyrics.

'I don't get it! It was here on top!'

Danny who was trying the piano out watched by Angel and Jemma who thought it must be great to be able to sit down and tinkle like that, wasn't too fussed.

'Not to worry, Speedy – we'll try one of the others.'

But Speedy was not to be so easily placated, and went on searching.

'It was the only one that really worked.'

PJ appeared on the half landing and bawled in their direction.

'Got a minute, Speedy?'

But Speedy was immersed.

'Busy.'

PJ wasn't to give up so easily.

'Got a little treat for you.'

Something in PJ's tone made Speedy sit up and pay attention. He said to Danny,

'Hang on. Back in a sec.'

As he went to the stairs, PJ raced ahead of him to warn the others, and Jemma slipped into Speedy's vacated seat next to Danny who was playing through the tune he and Speedy were going to work on,

'Can't you play something a bit livelier – that one sounds as though someone's died.'

'Okay – how about this.'

And with a smile Danny launched into a fast and beautiful classical piece.

The music filled Byker and a magical moment was underway. Angel and Jemma were entranced, Nicola who had just arrived, and gone to sit in one corner to chat with Charlie about Donna and her dad, stopped talking, and they both turned and listened wrapt. Even Alison came from the office so she could hear it more clearly. The piece only lasted maybe a minute and a half, but during that time everybody almost held their breath with the thrill of it. As he finished playing, Danny looked to Jemma and asked the question with a smile.

'Like that?'

Jemma shook her head.

'I was thinking more of Rock and Roll really.'

Upstairs in the committee room, Speedy, a bit bemused as to what was going on, had been sat in a chair, and the gang, battling to keep straight faces, took up their positions in front of him like a choir, with PJ at the centre playing the conductor.

'Ready, gang!' he called, and with one voice they replied:

'Ready!'

And then, taking a line each as PJ pointed at them, they let Speedy have it. Duncan first.

'I'm a lonely man.'

Then Kelly.

'Who walks a lonely road.'

Followed by Winston.

'Alone.'

It was as Tessa said the fourth line, 'Everyone needs someone to talk with,' that Speedy realised the awful truth. It was his lyrics they were saying at him.

Debbie was speaking as he started to rise.

'Everyone needs someone to walk with.'

And Duncan continued,

'But I'm a lonely man . . . '

But by the time Kelly got around to saying,

'Walking a lonely road,' Speedy was on the floor tussling with a laughing PJ trying to get the piece of paper out of his hand screaming, 'You're a ratbag, PJ! Give me it!'

By which time the whole gang was hooting with laughter.

Downstairs, Nicola had finally found a reasonable excuse to go across to Danny. As ever it was Jemma who was the convenient ploy.

'Jemma – Dad said you've got to go home for tea.'

'But . . . '

'No buts now!'

'Come on, Angel.'

And both, having said their goodbyes to Danny, grudgingly went.

Nicola was about to move off when, as she had hoped, Danny spoke.

'Hello again?'

She turned to look at him with a frown.

'Do I know you?'

'Dimmoro's café – lunch time.'

She feigned a return of memory.

'Oh yes. You were there having a barney with the Italian bloke.'

'My Uncle Paulo. And you were having a barney with your friend.'

Nicola laughed.

'As per usual.'

'Has she recovered her temper yet?'

'With Donna you never can tell.'

They both laughed again. Then Nicola played her ace.

'We're supposed to make new people feel welcome, so, fancy a coffee?'

'Sure.'

And with that they were on their way.

By the time Speedy returned in triumph with his lost lyric, the piano was once more deserted.

He looked at the bit of paper in his hand and decided it said it all. And with a chuckle he read it out loud to himself.

'I'm a lonely man.'

And then he too headed for a coffee.

Donna sat and stared at Jim, willing him to move. She had been at the hospital all evening, sitting silently beside Lisa simply looking at him and occasionally glancing at the monitor that confirmed his heart was still beating. He breathed, but it seemed as though his chest hardly moved in the process. He was deadly white, his face lifeless. Donna realised that at some point she had accepted the fact that various tubes were entering him, one up his nose, one feeding a drip into his arm, others going off carrying his blood for cleansing, and it no longer made her cringe. This was her dad. This was the man she loved. So, she had sat silent at his side the whole evening, and now Lisa had left the room for a few minutes, either for a coffee or to use the loo or whatever, Donna didn't know, hadn't asked, and hadn't cared. All she cared about was this man in front of her who she was willing to move.

Donna took his hand which lay on the coverlet. It was soft, dead, gave no sign of life, but she held it tight, as if to give herself comfort. And then she did a thing she could have only done without prying eyes watching her, she leant forward and spoke to him gently.

'I've talked to the doctor, Dad – it's not going to be easy but, when you come to – I'm going to let them take one of my kidneys and give it to you. You won't have to be on a machine for life. You understand?'

She waited momentarily to see whether there was any sign of him being aware of what she was saying. There wasn't.

Finally, she continued in an even gentler whisper than before, a little shy to be saying it out loud after all these years.

'I know I've never said it, Dad – because you don't; but . . . maybe, after that, you'll finally know . . . how much I love you.'

She had a massive lump in her throat that she thought would choke her, and she fought it back. And then a shock ran through her whole being as if she had been struck by lightning, as what happened, happened.

She had felt him squeeze her hand!

'Dad. Dad! Can you hear me?'

And she saw he was trying to raise his eyelids. He was hearing her.

'Dad! Can you hear me, Dad! Speak to me.' And then he was doing just that. No words came but his lips were moving, trying to make words. Donna saw the movement, and leant forward as close as she could get to him, her ear within an inch of his mouth all ready to catch any word, any slightest whisper. Again his lips moved.

'What is it, Dad? What are you trying to say?'

And finally the word came; the same word repeated twice, and it pierced Donna to the heart.

Her father said, in a tiny but unmistakable whisper.

'Lisa. Lisa?'

And then, with a sigh, once more he lapsed back into unconsciousness.

At that moment the door opened and Lisa was there. Without knowing it, Donna had a lone teardrop slowly trickling down her cheek. Her eyes wide with horror were fixed on Jim. Lisa saw the tear and the look, and knew something had happened.

'What is it, Donna?'

There was no reply.

'What is it?!'

Finally Donna found her voice.

Slowly and quietly she told it.

'He spoke. First he squeezed my hand, then his eyes fluttered; then he spoke.'

'What did he say?'

Donna let go of Jim's hand, then sat up straight in her chair. Finally she turned to face Lisa, and after a long pause, totally composed once more, she gave her reply.

'It was too quiet to hear.'

CHAPTER FIVE

Having kept an eye on the underpass all evening, and his mother not having arrived, Fraser had finally been drawn back to the bridge overlooking Cardboard City as if by a magnet.

As darkness had fallen fires were lit down there, and in their flickering flames he saw the drunks and derelicts meandering aimlessly clutching their bottles and shouting or screaming as the mood took them. In the distance a clock had chimed out a message that midnight had arrived, but still Fraser went on waiting.

At one point an old woman in a shabby black coat swayed drunkenly down the road towards him, her face hidden behind a tattered scarf. As she was about to walk past, Fraser stepped in front her.

'Is that you, Mam?'

The scarf fell away, and he saw not only that it wasn't his mother, but that he had frightened her by stopping her in that way.

'Sorry – thought you were someone else.' But too late, she had already scurried past with a little whimper of fear, and was quickly making her way down the path that led into what was for her the safety of Cardboard City, away from the young yobboes like Fraser who inhabited the outside world.

Lou was in her dressing gown, dozing in an armchair, when the slam of the front door startled her awake. A glance at the clock told her it was just after one in the morning.

Fraser, having parked his bike and hung his coat, finally opened the door and saw Lou waiting there, and knew why she hadn't gone to bed yet, even though it was well past her usual time.

He crossed glum-faced to slump into the chair opposite her before speaking.

'Want me to say it for you, Lou? Save you the effort?'

'Could try it.'

'Where have you been, Fraser; out till this time; no phone call; should be ashamed of yourself.'

Lou shifted to ease an ache as she spoke.

'And the rest. It's no fun worrying yourself silly while trying to keep a cheery face on so your sister doesn't worry herself silly.'

Fraser knew what she meant. That was a game he'd been playing every time he had seen Spuggie that day.

'Sorry, Lou. Bit of really bad news has crept into me life – and it's driving everything else out of me mind.'

As ever, her long worried wait was forgotten, and she was instantly ready to give support.

'Like to get it off your chest, pet?'

He saw the memory of what he was about to say in his mind's eye before he spoke.

'Couple of nights back, I went to the pictures with Spuggie. As I went through the underpass there was this old woman begging . . . '

At which point Spuggie in her dressing gown burst in from her room and launched into the attack.

'I thought it might be you! Where have you been, Fraser?! Out till this time; no phone call? Should be ashamed of yourself – Lou's been worried sick and trying to hide it so she didn't upset me!'

Fraser having had about enough for one evening lost his cool.

'Don't you start as well, Spuggie! I can really do without stereophonic nagging just at the moment!'

Before Spuggie could reply, Speedy's door also opened and he came to join them.

'I'm glad you're all up – I've just had this great idea for a song and I'd like to lay it on you.'

But by then Lou had had enough, and was standing all ready to go off.

'Enough! I'm ready for me bed even if you lot aren't! Come on! Let's have you out of here!'

And with that she was heading for the hallway ready to lock up. Speedy also went back to his room reading his lyric as he went.

Fraser hung back momentarily ready to appease Spuggie.

'Sorry to worry you.'

'Don't flatter yourself. Take more than you being out late to worry me.'

'Thanks, Spug. Nice to know you're wanted.'

And he too was heading for his room when Spuggie's question stopped him.

'So where you been?'

'Mind your own business.'

'Great! I shan't waste me time worrying about you again!'

Fraser smiled and said it gently.

''Night, Spug.'

And they both went on their way.

Having checked all was safely locked up Lou was heading for her room, when she noted the light shining under Robert's door.

She knocked lightly and looked in.

The crumpled bedclothes indicated that Robert had been in bed, but now he was sitting at the foot of the bed simply looking out of the window into the night-time park. Lou closed the door behind her and went to sit alongside him.

'What is it?'

There was a moment's pause and then he took a folded letter out of his pyjama pocket and passed it to her without speaking.

She opened it and quickly read it. Robert had got his place in the specialist hospital. He would have to leave and go down south to live. Lou looked at him sadly.

'When did you get it?'

'Yesterday afternoon.'

'We'll miss you, you know?'

'Aye. And I'll miss you lot, though you'd never guess it from the way I've been lately.'

Lou could have lied at that point, but it wasn't her way. Instead she shifted the subject.

'When you going to tell Charlie?'

That was exactly what Robert had been sitting at his window pondering. Having made his mind up he turned to tell her.

'Tomorrow.'

Lisa lay by herself in the double bed, in her and Jim's bedroom, directly above the main bar of the pub, fast asleep. Moonlight shone through the half open curtains bathing her in its pallid light. She looked vulnerable. Her face softened with sleep, had temporarily lost the look of worry it had worn ever since the moment of Jim's fall. As the clock on the bedside table ticked towards two, the handle of the bedroom door quietly turned, and then without a sound the door slowly opened. The figure who had entered, and could not be seen in the half light of that side of the room, carefully crossed on tiptoe to stand and look down at Lisa sleeping in the bed. Lisa, as the figure cut the moonlight from her face, sensed she was being watched and was in an instant wide awake and alert. The figure had moved so close to the bed that it too was now lit by moonlight.

Lisa saw that it was Donna who looked down on her.

But this was a Donna she had never seen before. A Donna wracked with silent sobs, her face awash with the tears that continued to flow as Lisa looked at her.

There was only one thing to do in the face of such a depth of sorrow, and Lisa did it. She opened her arms, and Donna without hesitation took the offer, and went to be wrapped by them. As Lisa cuddled Donna to her, like a baby, she whispered, placating.

'Don't worry, love. He's going to be all right; you just wait, he's going to be fine.'

And struggling against her distress Donna finally got the words out.

'It's not that!'

'Then what is it?'

'I've done something so awful – so really awful . . . I didn't think even I could stoop so low.'

'Tell me. It can't be that bad.'

Donna's tears were flowing once more.

'But it is!'

'Tell me.'

Donna pulled slightly away, and almost got control again.

'Last night, when Dad spoke at the hospital, and I said . . . and I said I couldn't hear what he said.'

'Yes.'

'Well I did hear.'

And with a sob she was out of control again.

'What did he say, Donna? What did Jim say?'

And finally, Donna managed to get it off her chest.

'He said . . . "Lisa . . . Lisa."'

And then she was back in Lisa's arms heartbroken and ashamed.

Sure that wrapped in her arms as she was, Donna could not see her, Lisa gave a sad smile, and then softly spoke the words that shocked Donna so much she sat bolt upright once again.

'That's really nice of you, Donna. Thank you.'

Donna could not believe she had heard what she had heard.

'What?'

'Really nice of you. You must have known how bad I'd feel if Jim was asking for me and I wasn't there. That was really kind. Thanks.'

And Donna knowing what her real motive had been, and knowing that Lisa must also know, and totally shattered by this act of both kindness and forgiveness, was in floods once again.

That morning Debbie came from her bedroom, her eyes clouded with sleep and staggered to the bathroom door, and started banging on it.

'Come on, Jemma, you've been there long enough! Jemma!'

She decided this time she was not going to give up so easily and kept pummelling even though she was getting no response at all. If she had turned round and looked towards the kitchen she would have seen why.

Jemma and Angel were stood at the doorway there, both standing on one leg, Long John Silver fashion, and were watching her amazed.

Debbie paused in her banging to shout.

'Jemma! Come on! At least have the good manners to answer me! What are you playing at this morning! A mute! Jemma! Will you open this door!'

Jemma and Angel exchanged a glance that without a word being spoken clearly said, 'Aren't big sisters potty.'

And as Debbie called once more, 'For the last time, Jemma! Open this door!' Jemma hopped in that direction, in front of the amazed Debbie, opened the door which wasn't locked, and said brightly:

'There you go.'

And then she hopped back to Angel, and both hopped off into the kitchen once more.

In spite of his late night Fraser arrived at Byker dead on the dot of eight-thirty. Geoff was nowhere to be seen. It was in fact fifteen minutes later that he arrived, parked the car, and spoke as he crossed to where Fraser waited.

'Sorry I'm late, Fraser – road works.'

Fraser had to smile.

'I didn't say a word, Geoff.'

Geoff's reply was friendly enough.

'Your smug look is saying it all for you, Fraser.'

Fraser laughed; he was looking forward to this day's work. If he had known then what the day actually had in store for them both, he wouldn't have been quite so jolly.

Spuggie ignored her breakfast as she played a needle match at the fastest speed with her computer chess set. She couldn't believe it when the machine made its next move.

Checkmate.

'How could you do that to me, you stupid electronic ratbag!'

Speedy still in his pyjamas wandered through clutching the writing pad which was now never seen to leave his side. In passing he threw the question at Spuggie.

'Any idea what rhymes with orange, Spug?'

She forgot her problem for a moment while she thought about it.

'Porridge?'

Speedy looked at her with disdain.

'That's not a rhyme!'

'Don't grumble at me; it's you who's supposed to be the poet.'

Speedy was quick to defend his true title.

'Lyricist, not poet.'

'What's the difference?' Spuggie asked, interested.

'Apparently a half a million quid if you get the right one.'

'Well I wouldn't hold your breath, Speedy. Can't see you getting a long way up the charts with songs about oranges and porridge.'

As Speedy disappeared, and Spuggie started to set the chess pieces up once more, it was Robert's turn to come in. He crossed to sit at the table opposite her. Spuggie looked up and he smiled at her as he spoke.

'Morning, Spuggie.'

Spuggie's reaction was immediate and over the top.

'Oh no! Has someone told you I'm going to die!'

Robert was suitably bemused.

'What do you mean?'

'You've just been nice to me! First time for weeks! You know something about me health I don't, don't you! Quick! Tell me! How long have I got left to live, Robert?!'

He had to smile ruefully at the thought.

'Have I been as bad as that?'

Spuggie went back to setting up her chess pieces.

'Worse – you've been a major pain in the bum for yonks now.'

Robert said it quietly.

'I'm leaving.'

Spuggie was surprised.

'You've only just come in.'

'No. I'm leaving here. The Gallaghers'.'

At which Robert had all her attention. Feeling the way she did about it, the worst thing in the world was to have to leave the Gallaghers'.

Neither of them had noticed that Speedy had come back into the room and was listening to what was being said.

'Oh no! You poor thing! What happened? – Has Lou thrown you out for being such a misery?'

Again Robert had to smile.

'My decision. I have to go away for treatment. But I need some advice – from a woman.'

Spuggie tried not to glow at the thought of Robert calling her a woman, but failed. He did have the good grace to ignore her blush.

'The thing I want to know, Spuggie, is – how do I best break the news to Charlie?'

As she considered her reply, Speedy slipped out of the room thrilled. With Robert gone the field was clear. Charlie wouldn't have a boyfriend any more.

High on Byker roof, all the tools and materials were gathered together all ready for the job to be got underway.

Geoff looked at the place they were going to have to climb to, and then turned to Fraser to ask the obvious.

'How's your head for heights?'

'No problem.'

Fraser peered down from the parapet to the dizzying drop below.

'Like me to walk round the edge of the parapet to prove the point?'

'I'll take your word.'

And with that Geoff was over the back wall and heading for the area where the work needed doing, carrying a bag of tools, and the length of rope he was going to tie himself off with in a loop over his shoulder. It was a bit of a dodgy climb to reach the starting point, Fraser decided. When he had done it a couple of days back he hadn't been loaded down with gear like he was now. When they finally arrived where they were heading, they were about as far as you could go on the roof without falling off the other side.

They had reached a flat section that Geoff had decided they were going to work from. Then Geoff made a harness of the rope he carried, put it round his chest, and then, having measured off the length he would need to safely work on, he firmly tied the other end of the rope off to an old iron ring that was bolted into the floor up there, probably for that very purpose.

'Rope strong enough to take your weight?'

'Aye, no problem, and yours too come to that. But the thing to do is make sure it doesn't come to that.'

And having given the rope a good tug, he was all ready to lean over the low edge, and have a look at the damage on the pipe below the roof line. 'Okay, stand by, Fraser. I'm about to go over and have a look, your job's to keep my feet on the ground this side, right?'

And Fraser crossed to him all ready to hold on to his legs, as Geoff looked over to assess the damage.

As soon as Speedy was sure he had the room to himself he questioned Lou about Robert's departure.

'Why's he going?'

'He's going because he feels he has to go. Extra treatment. Besides which – "A man's got to do what a man's got to do."'

Speedy asked the next question carefully.

'You think he'll be back?'

Lou doubted it.

'Be unusual. When my chicks leave this nest they're usually well launched.' She was watching Speedy quite closely, trying to find a clue as to why he was so interested, and then she had a stab at it.

'You're in love with Charlie, Speedy, aren't you?'

His blush gave the lie to what his lips said.

'What makes you think that?'

Lou was not only not fooled, but had already found the evidence days ago.

'I dust your room on the odd occasion, Speedy. Don't need to be a Sherlock Holmes to find your favourite photograph just at the moment.'

He saw there was no point in keeping up the pretence.

'Yes, I am.'

Lou shook her head in a warning.

'You go careful, just because Charlie is now Robert's *yesterday*; don't think there's any guarantee she might be your *tomorrow*. If there's anything more useless than *yesterday's dreams*, it's the *tuppenny daydreams* that follow.'

As she spoke Speedy watched her progressively wide-eyed. He thought he'd never heard such a wonderful little speech in his life. He quickly got his pen out and started writing it in his pad.

She watched him a while before speaking.

'What is it, Speedy, turning into a reporter now?'

He continued to write as he spoke.

'Lou – those words are wonderful.'

Which bemused her totally.

'What words?'

Speedy didn't reply, but stood, gave her a peck on the head, and headed for his room to get his latest song underway. Having gone in there, he immediately popped his head out again.

'What's a "tuppenny", Lou?'

She laughed.

'Kids know nowt these days. Comes from the old two pence coin – means not worth much.'

'Tuppenny! Wonderful word!'

And with that he was gone again.

Geoff tried to reach the pipe by leaning over the low wall of brickwork, while Fraser was hanging on to his legs. He couldn't reach, and Geoff saw he was going to have to try a different tack.

'I'm going to have to climb over, if I'm to reach it, Fraser.'

'Isn't that a bit dodgy?'

'There's a wastepipe I can stand on, looks solid enough. The rope's secure, should it be needed, and you can hang on to me arm.'

With that Geoff was going over, his legs momentarily in space till he found his foothold on the wastepipe.

Fraser was suddenly very worried. While he was hanging on grimly to Geoff's arm, he was looking down on the drop below. If the small pipe Geoff was standing on should break, all that was left between Geoff and a massive drop was the rope.

'I think it's a scaffolding job really, Geoff.'

Geoff was already a bit winded from his efforts.

'I *know* it's a scaffolding job, Fraser. But we haven't got scaffolding money.'

Seeing that Fraser really was worried, Geoff continued: 'I'll be all right. Should be able to get it from here. We'll have it patched in no time.'

As Fraser hung on to his arm, and Geoff reached down to feel for the broken section of pipe, the rope around Geoff's middle was totally taut, and pulling against the strong iron ring that it was fastened to. When Fraser had asked the question earlier, was the rope strong enough, Geoff had answered truly enough, yes it was. The iron ring also was immensely strong. What neither of them had known was that the fixings of the four bolts that held the iron ring were rotted. Unknown to either Geoff or Fraser, two of the bolts had already pulled out of their seating on the roof, and that a third bolt was about to do so if there was any additional pressure brought to bear. As Geoff walked a little further along the pipe he was standing on, putting even more strain on the rope, the pressure was applied, and the third bolt popped out.

Geoff, all unbeknowing now had just one bolt, and Fraser's armhold, as the only defence against a long, unbroken drop to the ground below, and almost certain death.

At the Gallaghers' Jemma and Angel were in the kitchen practising an act they hoped to do for the show at Byker. They were cross juggling with two apples and two oranges, the fruit going from Jemma's hands to Angel's and back again in a curve, a trick which wasn't made any easier by the fact that both of them were still standing on one leg.

Alan had popped his head round the door at one point and saw what was going on.

'How many times do I have to tell you – don't play with your food!'

Jemma turned to look at him.

'Sorry, Dad.'

But as is the way of things when you're juggling, if you lose your concentration the balls keep coming. In quick succession Jemma was hit on the head by two apples and two oranges. She looked round and a blushing Angel apologised nicely.

'Sorry, Jemma.'

Having picked up the fruit and put it back in the bowl, they hopped to the front room, and Jemma was the first to see, high above the surrounding trees, Fraser on Byker roof, hanging on to something.

At the moment that Jemma looked from the window, Fraser was finding it very tough going clinging on to Geoff's arm.

'How's it going, Geoff?! Me arm's just about to die on me!'

Geoff realised that Fraser was putting a lot of effort into it.

'I think you can give yourself a break for a few minutes now, Fraser. You can let go, I'm safe enough.'

Fraser wasn't too keen on that so he lied.

'Naw, it's all right. Not that bad. I'll survive.'

And Geoff knew he lied.

'Right, Fraser. That's an order. Let go your hold.'

'Are you sure?'

'Absolutely – safe as houses at the moment.'

And at that moment two things happened in quick succession to prove him wrong. The wastepipe beneath his feet snapped from his weight and fell away to the ground below, and the same second as the extra weight fell on it, the last bolt pulled from its bedding and the rope and iron ring that was holding Geoff was holding him no more, but shooting over Fraser's head to end up swinging far below Geoff's feet.

Fraser had instantly taken the whole of Geoff's weight and screamed with the pain of it, and Geoff scrabbling to get one fingertip hold on the brickwork was left dangling.

Fraser found the strength to scream it.

'Geoff, you're too heavy!! I can't hold you, man!! I can't hold you!!!'

Indeed the weight of Geoff was slowly pulling him over the edge as well, and looking down he could see Geoff's feet fighting to get a foothold, while swinging backwards and forwards over the drop to the concrete courtyard far below.

Fraser realised with horror, that as he couldn't let go no matter what, when Geoff finally went, as he surely must, he also would be dragged with him, and both of them were going to die a very bloody death indeed.

CHAPTER SIX

Jemma and Angel watched the unfolding drama at Byker, while standing one-legged at the window. It was Angel who had finally recognised the dangling man as Geoff, and it was she who asked the question.

'What do you think they're up to?'

Having thought about it fractionally Jemma had the answer.

'Probably practising their act for the show.' At that moment, luckily, Debbie entered the room and crossed to see what they were both staring at in such an interested fashion. What she saw made her scream the one word at the top of her voice.

'Dad!'

Alan knew how to recognise real trouble when he heard it and he instantly dropped what he was doing and came running.

One glance out of the window where Debbie pointed, then he was running off for the front door with Debbie in hot pursuit. Jemma and Angel exchanged a glance that soundlessly carried the question, 'So what's got into them.' Then both shrugged their shoulders and carried on watching Geoff swinging from side to side, like a pendulum on a grandfather clock.

There used to be a passage through the broken back fence at the Dobsons', straight into the Grove grounds, but Alan had recently mended it, putting new planks up. Now, with the axe he had grabbed in passing from the chopping block in the garden, he was smashing at it viciously. With three hefty blows he had chopped a way through, and he and Debbie were through it and running as fast as they could across the greenery for the Grove.

As they reached the building Debbie was fractionally ahead, and slammed through the door and was heading up the stairs as fast as she could go, with Alan close behind her.

Fraser's arms were burning with pain and nearly out of their sockets, he was sobbing bitterly with the agony of it, and Geoff also near to tears was trying to get a better hold with his hand and failing miserably. Even if he had found a good grip, he knew he had no strength left to pull himself up. He was just trying to work out how he could get free of Fraser's grip, so that Fraser wasn't also pulled to his death when Geoff let go, which he knew he soon must do as the agony was too great to bear much longer, when the door to the roof slammed open, and to his amazement he heard Debbie shouting.

'Hang on! We're coming!!'

And then the door slammed open again and he knew a second person had arrived.

Fraser, through his tears had not heard, so he was startled beyond belief, to see Debbie arrive at his side, lean over and clutch at Geoff's other arm, and was immediately hanging on just as desperately as Fraser was. It was Alan who managed to finally pull Geoff in, and the four of them fell in a heap on the flat surface where the morning's work had started in the first place, gasping for breath, and in Fraser's case still quietly crying and holding his right arm nursing the intense hurt.

After a long pause it was Alan who broke the silence, directing his remark at Geoff.

'Been hanging around long, have you?'

There was a slight pause, and then as the gag sunk in and the tension broke, all four of them burst out laughing, and the laughter went on and on.

Not knowing the drama that had been played out, other lives went on pretty much as normal. Upstairs at the Bell pub Donna made a telephone call while nearby Lisa sipped at her early morning coffee and listened to her getting progressively angry as the conversation continued.

'Look, I've just got to get hold of her! ... Because she's me mam and I need to talk to her! ... How long ago? ... Surely she must have left some forwarding address? ... Look – don't go talking about me mam like that! ... And you too!!'

And with that Donna slammed the phone down angrily.

'She's only gone and left her stupid boyfriend, hasn't she! Now, of all times! Does she ring me, tell me where I can find my mother if I need her desperately?! Not her, no. Just off without a word.'

Lisa put her cup down before speaking.

'My turn for confession?'

'You know where Mam is ?!'

'Sorry, no. But I did know she'd left her boyfriend. First thing I did was to try to let her know the news about Jim.'

Donna couldn't understand it.

'Why didn't you tell me? Save me having to talk to that oaf?'

Lisa smiled.

'Think about it.'

Which Donna did.

'I wouldn't have taken your word for it?'

'Something like that, yes.'

Donna slumped at the breakfast table defeated.

'I don't know what to do next, Lisa. I've got to get her permission otherwise they won't even consider me being a donor.'

Lisa asked the question carefully.

'Why you so dead set on doing this thing, Donna?'

Donna looked at Lisa warily. Then realising she wasn't just setting out to rile her, answered truthfully.

'You've seen what I'm like. You know I am not necessarily the first person who would go out of their way to do a good deed for another person.'

Again Lisa gave the merest glimmer of a smile.

'I may have got just a hint of the fact occasionally.'

Donna paused before continuing, it was a big admission she was about to make, and it was something she herself had only come to realise in the last couple of days.

'When it comes to Dad it's something else again. He doesn't know it, but if it came to a choice of dying so he could live, or going on living with him dead, there's no choice, Lisa. I'd give my life for Dad without hesitation – for what would life be without him?'

Lisa knew then that Donna had gone through the watershed of suffering as a child, and come out the other side a woman. And now, even though she didn't think it was the right thing for Donna to be doing, she would do everything in her power to help her. If Donna wanted to donate a kidney, and succeeded, that was to be her decision, and Lisa would no longer stand in her way.

'You know I'm not exactly "for" this plan your considering,

Donna, but I do think it would be a good idea if you heard it from your mother as well.'

'That's what I'm trying to organise but Polly's gone!'

Once more Lisa smiled.

'I think I do know how to get her back again.'

'How?'

And when Lisa told her, Donna had to admit it was a brilliant plan.

Danny and Speedy sat in Dimmoro's coffee bar with coffees in front of them once more. Danny sat patiently while Speedy as ever went on too long.

'It was Lou who gave me the idea – something she said.'

'Great.'

'I'd finished in no time.'

Having got to this point in the conversation at least twice before, Danny decided to push it on a bit.

'Do I finally get to see this number or not?'

Embarrassed, Speedy dug into his pocket for the piece of paper he had written the words on.

'Yeh, sure.'

Finding it he straightened it out, and then, still hesitant he passed it to Danny.

He decided it was a bit like handing a baby over, letting someone read your words for the first time. He chatted on nervously to cover his embarrassment.

'Not very well written out – I did it in a hurry . . . '

Danny's face was giving no hint as to what he thought as he read on.

' . . . I mean if it's no good, don't be embarrassed to say.'

Danny paused in his reading and looked up. 'Speedy, man, give me a break. Just let me read it, okay?'

Speedy picked up his cup nervously.

'Okay. Sorry.'

And sipped while Danny continued to read.

Finally Danny looked at Speedy again.

'What's a tuppenny?'

'Old coin not worth much.'

'Oh.'

And then he again read on, Speedy watching anxiously. Having finished Danny folded the sheet of paper.

'It works with the tune I gave you.'

Speedy slightly bemused, looked across to the closed piano.

'How can you tell?'

Danny smiled.

'Same way you obviously did, I hear it in my head. The only difference is I get the whole orchestra playing along with it.'

Speedy thought what a great talent that must be.

'Amazing.'

'No more amazing than what you've done.'

Speedy felt himself flush at what must obviously be a compliment.

'You mean it?'

Danny once more looked at the paper but this time read out loud from it.

'"How many tuppenny daydreams – please tell me honestly, friend – how many tuppenny daydreams – Before the nightmare can end."'

This was the first time Speedy had heard Danny speak his words, and he was quietly chuffed as to how nice they sounded, but there was nothing he could say. Danny broke the ensuing silence.

'How about if we go see if we can find ourselves a singer?'

Speedy glugged his coffee down as he spoke. 'Great! Charlie'll be at Byker.'

Danny was surprised.

'On a Saturday?'

Speedy remembered the call that Robert had made fixing the date, and was a bit ashamed of himself, knowing what Robert was going to say to her, for feeling so thrilled about it.

'I heard someone phoning her, saying to be there. She'll be there.'

Danny also finished his coffee and stood.

'So what we waiting for?'

And with that they were off.

Geoff was sitting waiting patiently in the casualty department of the hospital for Fraser to be cleared. Luckily, when they had arrived there, it hadn't been too busy, and Geoff had soon been checked out and given the all clear. They had found that apart from the odd scratch, no damage had been done. Now he was waiting anxiously for Fraser to arrive back from the X-ray department where he had been sent to have his damage assessed. Geoff knew that a man of his weight must have put an enormous strain on the arms of somebody as slight as Fraser. As he thought back to it, on reflection, he could not work out how Fraser had managed to hang on for so long.

Just at that moment, Fraser came through the swing doors and into the waiting area. He saw Geoff and crossed to him. Geoff spoke the one word as he approached, as ever hiding his worry behind gruffness.

'Well?'

Fraser indicated his right hand and arm.

'Nothing broken. Bit sprained and bruised is all.'

Geoff stood pleased.

'That's great news.'

As they headed for the exit Fraser told him the rest of it.

'They suggested I take it easy for the day, case there's any after-shock or summat.'

'We'll get you in the car, and I'll drive you home to bed then.'

'Naw, it's all right, Geoff man, I can get the bus.'

Geoff stopped and looked at him.

Fraser wondered why his face had suddenly gone so serious.

'What is it Geoff?'

'Fraser – you miss the point or haven't got it yet.'

Fraser was a bit thrown. He could never remember ever seeing Geoff quite this serious before except when telling someone off. But as Geoff carried on speaking he began to see what he was getting it.

'I owe my life to you, son. There's not many ways one can balance the books on something like that, but if anything crops up, anything, you only have to ask.'

Fraser was suitably chuffed and embarrassed all at the same time.

'Well . . . right, Geoff. Thanks, man.'

'No, thank you, Fraser.'

And with that Geoff put his hand out to be shook, and Fraser without thinking about it, took it, and it was only as Geoff squeezed it firmly, that, too late, Fraser remembered it was his bad hand, and as he ended up on his knees on the floor screaming, Geoff realised it also.

In the committee room the gang stood round the star of the afternoon, PJ's unicycle. Along with PJ, Winston, Kelly, Duncan and Tessa were there, plus a few younger kids who had arrived in the hope of some laughs at the big kids' expense.

It was PJ who broke the silence.

'So what do you reckon?'

And Duncan who answered,

'Just get on it and go for it, PJ.'

There was laughter as Tessa said it for all of them.

'What you got to lose except your life?'

'Thanks for that kind thought, Tessa.'

At which point Debbie burst in full of it.

'Hey! Have you all heard yet!? I saved Geoff's life!'

Winston got the reply out first.

'We've heard! And it wasn't just you: Fraser's been declared hero of the day.'

Everybody agreed, then PJ quickly chipped in.

'We've done Geoff's drama to the death, Debbie. Now it's the turn of me and me unicycle.'

Duncan was getting a bit bored with lots of build-up and no drama.

'Get a move on, PJ. Me and Tessa are due to saw Jemma and Angel in half in about five minutes.'

Debbie couldn't wait.

'Go and do it now, we'll manage without you.'

But Duncan wasn't having that.

'I want to see him try it!'

And now they were all insisting that PJ should get on with it.

'Okay, okay! Just want to think about it a bit. I still say the stupid machine should have handlebars.'

And with that he prepared to mount.

'Who has the instructions?'

That was Kelly's job.

'I have.'

'Okay so read it.'

And she did.

'Hold the bicycle at an angle behind you with the saddle pointing forward.'

He did so.

'Put the saddle under your behind.'

It was Winston who threw in the gag that caused general laughter.

'Being careful not to damage the equipment.'

'Don't worry yourself, Winston. I'm going very careful. Don't want to end up as the very first unicycle eunuch!'

Which caused even more mirth.

Kelly continued to call through the hilarity.

'Foot on the higher pedal.'

'Right, done that.'

'Now all you've got to do, it says, is push down and then keep pedalling.'

Which PJ did, and having swung round in a perfect circle started travelling backwards at speed before crashing into a wall and falling in a heap, Tom and Jerry fashion, much to everyone's glee.

As the roar went up upstairs, Charlie was sat at the piano downstairs chatting with Danny as they waited for Speedy to come from the coffee bar with drinks for them all.

Donna walking in the front door saw her, and crossed in that direction.

'Seen PJ, Charlie?'

'Let me introduce you to Danny Dim . . . '

But Donna didn't have time for the sociability.

'Another time. Bit of a rush. PJ?'

It was Jemma, sitting with Angel on a small coffin nearby, who having clearly heard the question called the answer.

'He's upstairs with the mob.'

And Donna without even a nod of appreciation in her direction, headed for the stairs.

Angel was somewhat shocked at her ill-manners.

'Doesn't she know about Mr Thank You?' Jemma said it disdainfully.

'She doesn't know owt except "Miss Donna".

Danny was equally surprised by the young woman's curtness.

'So who was that?' he asked Charlie.

'That was Donna – man-eater by trade.'

Danny smiled at the thought.

'Obviously off her food just at the moment.'

And they both laughed.

Arriving at the committee room, Donna opened the door just in time to let a well-out-of-control PJ come riding out of the room to miss her by inches, and then go crashing into the banisters before finally falling in a heap with his bike on the landing. Donna crossed to look at him, as the rest of the gang also came out to stare.

'Well I've heard of people throwing themselves at each other, PJ, but this is going a bit far even for you.'

PJ spoke while getting himself up and disentangled.

'Donna, I promise this will never happen again, the last person I want to throw myself at is the nasty ... '

She butted in before he could add the expected tag 'Donna Bell'.

'Peace pact, PJ, I need your help.'

He couldn't believe he was hearing correctly.

'*You* need *my* help?'

'That's right. Lisa's idea. I've got a favour to ask that's right up your street.'

While their conversation continued on the landing with Debbie keeping a jealous eye on them both from the distance, Duncan and Tessa slipped off, saw in hand, to sort out Jemma and Angel.

Speedy arrived from the tea bar with the three cups of coffee, calling to Danny and Charlie as he approached.

'Here we go, you guys – now can we work?'

Charlie smiled at the greeting.

'This guy's ready when you are.'

Then picked up the sheet of paper off the piano and glanced at it again.

'So what's a tuppenny, Speedy?'

As Speedy was telling her, near them Duncan and Tessa were helping to get Jemma and Angel into the strange double coffin that Geoff had organised for them the day before.

The two girls had to take their shoes off, and then climb in and lie side by side 'top to tail' fashion. Jemma's head coming through one hole, and Angel's feet coming through another hole at the same end; while Angel's head, and Jemma's feet came out of holes at the other end.

They were both in and Tessa and Duncan were putting the lid back on, when Jemma made her loud complaint, and pulled the face to go with it.

'Angel! Your feet are foul! They really pong!'

Angel at the far end was suitably disbelieving.

'They can't pong! I only washed them last Sunday!'

'Sunday! That was days ago!'

It was Duncan who broke up the battle.

'Come on, you two, keep it down! This is supposed to be serious.'

'So is having your nose murdered by toes!' Jemma retorted.

'That's rude!' shouted Angel from the far end.

Having finally got them quietened down, Duncan got the saw all ready to start chopping them in half, when he remembered something.

'Get the bucket, Tessa.'

'Oh yes. Forgetting.'

As Tessa went off to the kitchen, Danny started playing the piano and Charlie soared into song.

Speedy sat quietly thrilled at the sound they were both making. He could hardly believe they were his words she was singing, but they were. Danny pulled her up on a tricky bit.

'No, no! It's . . . '

He played the two notes on the piano and sang the word.

'Day . . . light.'

She sang it again, and got it dead on the button.

'Day . . . light.'

Danny was pleased.

'Great! And again.'
Once more she sang it.
'Day . . . light.'
Again perfect.
As they continued to work through the song Tessa arrived back with the bucket, put it under the coffin, and then Duncan started to saw. The raucous noise cut through the singing, and Danny stopped playing. It was an irritated Speedy who said it for the three of them.
'Hey, come on, Duncan man! Give us a break! We're trying out a song for the show.'
Duncan paused in his exertions.
'What you think we're doing here, Speedy, making firewood?'

As Duncan and Speedy shouted at each other, Debbie coming down the stairs saw Jemma's feet sticking out alongside Angel's head. Being careful that Angel couldn't see her, she got in a position where she could tickle the feet without being seen.
Immediately Jemma was in gales of hysterical giggles and fighting to get her feet out of the hole. Tessa asked her the question.
'What is it?'
And Jemma had no doubt.
'Angel's tickling my feet!'
But Angel protested quite rightly.
'How could I?'
By the time Duncan and Tessa got to look Debbie had nipped back up the stairs, and peered down laughing from the balcony. Duncan confirmed what Angel had said.
'Angel's right, Jemma; she couldn't have done it!'

Speedy meanwhile was still keen to sort the clash of interest.
'Can't you move away a bit, Duncan?'
Tessa who didn't want the fun to turn into battlefield stuff came up with the solution.
'Let's move by the door, Dunc.'
He was agreeable enough.
'Okay.'

The coffin which was on two small trolleys with wheels would be easy enough to move over there.

'Ready when you are, Tessa.'

And with that, as the singing got underway again, they were pushing the trolleys and coffin on top of it, along with its contents, to the doorway.

In seconds Duncan was sawing again, but Tessa stopped him.

'Hang on! Bucket!'

'Oh yeh.' As she set off he called;

'Bring the two sliders back with you as well!'

Having got the bucket and the two sliders, which were simply squares of wood that would slot into the hole at the middle when Duncan had finished sawing, Tessa brought them back. Putting the bucket underneath the coffin, she nodded at Duncan and he started to saw once more. And soon the coffin was in two halves.' The squares of wood slotted in, and then came the best bit. Tessa pulled one trolley towards her, and Duncan pulled the other towards him, and the various halves of Jemma and Angel were a metre apart!

It was Duncan who asked the question.

'You both okay?'

And the cheery reply came back from both.

'Fine.' With Jemma adding, 'Now what?'

'At that point,' said Duncan as much to remind Tessa as anything else, 'we do the test to see that the nerve endings are still intact. You tickle Angel's feet, Tessa and I'll do Jemma's.'

At which point they both did and Angel and Jemma laughed uproariously but protesting as they did so.

Jemma saying. 'Oh no! Stop it, Tessa! Stop!

While Angel shouted. 'Oh no, Duncan! Stop! Stop it!'

The tickling test being finished the laughter died away.

'Brilliant! perfect timing.'

Tessa asked, 'What then?'

'Then,' said Duncan, 'together we turn them both in to face the room to prove they both really are well and truly in two halves.' And as Angel and Jemma were turned, feet still sticking out beside their heads, which were now along side each other, they spoke from their positions about a metre apart.

'Watcha, Angel!'

'Hiya, Jem!'

Duncan and Tessa were thrilled that it had gone so well at the first attempt. They shook hands pleased. Then Duncan dropped a small bombshell. 'Terrific! Back in a minute the pair of you. Got to pop to the loo.'

Jemma and Angel couldn't believe it when Tessa followed suit.

'Me too. Must be all the excitement.'

And both called out together as Duncan and Tessa disappeared:

'But what about us!'

But too late they had gone.

Charlie had just finished the song for the second time when Robert came in through the front door. Angel and Jemma exchanged a glance as he stood between them without noticing that they were there.

Glancing around Robert saw Charlie sitting with Danny and Speedy and his face darkened. Danny made a joke and Charlie's laugh drifted across the room to him like a tinkling challenge.

At the same moment that Robert had arrived, Donna, having got PJ to agree to help her with her project to contact her mum, had come strolling down the stairs, and seeing the little drama being played out, crossed to stand with Robert between the two halves of Angel and Jemma.

She turned to look at the view that Robert was scowling at, and could not resist the comment.

'And so life goes on, aye Robert?'

He gave her a hard look, but his attention was immediately distracted by Jemma's comment.

'You do both realise we can see right up your noses, don't you?'

For the first time Donna and Robert noticed Jemma and Angel.

'Good job we're not frightened of bogies!' said Angel, and with that, Angel and Jemma both cracked up.

Donna then left, but Robert was still standing there ignoring the young girls' loud hoots of laughter, when Speedy finally saw him staring in their direction blackly.

He said. 'Friend of yours is here, Charlie.'

As she looked in that direction, Robert had set off for the tea bar.

'And yours too, surely?'

Speedy's reply was a cold rebuttal.

'Not after what he said to me the last time we spoke.'

Much to Danny's amazement, Charlie was up on her feet, and heading for the tea bar. 'Hey Charlie! Where you off? It's a working session.'

But she ignored him and continued on her way.

Speedy explained the score with a voice well oiled with bitterness.

'Not any more it's not, Danny. The session's over. "Mr Wonderful" has arrived.'

Jemma saw Duncan and Tessa approaching and chatting on together nonchalantly, and called out to them.

'Where you both been! We could have bled to death for all you care!'

Angel added, 'We passed the time counting the hairs up Donna's nose. Very boring.'

Having calmed them down, Duncan and Tessa got the halves of coffin back the right way round and together again. Took the sliders out of the middle, and then lifted the lid, which was now also in two halves, off together. Then with a mutual gasp they slapped the lid back on again.

Jemma was alarmed.

'What is it?'

It was Duncan who told her.

'Some bad news I'm afraid.'

They both asked what in unison.

Duncan's face was very serious.

'You want to tell them, Tessa?'

She was equally serious.

'No, I think you better – you're the magician.'

'Okay. Sorry. It hasn't worked.'

Jemma was adamant.
'Course it worked perfectly! We were in two halves.'
And then Duncan dropped the bombshell.
'Yes, but the problem is, you both still are. Sorry.'
Their screams of rage could be heard throughout the Grove.

In the tea bar Charlie was trying to talk some sense into Robert who was sulking into his coffee.
'Come on, Robert, what is it with you at the moment? After days you ring me out of the blue to meet you here, I change my arrangements so I can make it, and now you sit scowling into your coffee.'
He lashed it at her.
'Well what do you expect! I came to see you, not you and some blue-eyed boyfriend.'
Charlie was staggered.
'Are you crazy? I'd never even seen the bloke till half an hour ago. He's a mate of Speedy!'
Though proved wrong Robert wouldn't give up on it.
'You're getting along well enough.'
Charlie stood truly furious at his childish jealousy.
'This is pathetic! Truly pathetic! I never thought I'd see the day when you'd get to the point of being such a . . . '
She looked for the right word. Rejected 'Wimp' as being too weak, and then found the word. It was a word that not only would she come to regret using forever, but a word that would keep her awake nights as she hated herself for having said it. The word she angrily spat at him was,
' . . . Cripplehead!!'

It was as if she'd physically slapped him across the face. Before the word had echoed away she was already apologising.
'No, Robert! That wasn't what I intended to say!'
But it was too late. Robert stood, and trying to gather whatever remaining dignity he could around him, replied bitterly.
'But that is what you said, Charlie. That is what you said.'
And with that, he walked slowly and painfully to the door, she presumed to exit out of the room and out of her life forever.

Later, as Angel and Jemma walked home together, down the path that led to Byker Grove's front gate, they talked about the tease they had had to put up with. Angel reckoned that Tessa and Duncan must have planned the wind-up when they were off at the loo together, for a laugh.

'Oh yes! Ending up in two halves for the rest of our lives, very funny!'

But Angel hushed her. There was a creepy-looking boy coming up the drive towards them. They weren't to know it, but it was the beggar boy, Lee. As they approached he called to them.

'Excuse me, can you tell me if Fraser's in there today?'

Angel said it as an aside to Jemma.

'Remember what your mam said about not talking to strange blokes?'

Jemma certainly did, and added, 'And they don't come much stranger, do they!'

He drew level with them, and directed his remark at Jemma.

'Fraser in there?'

'No. He nearly died, so he's gone to bed.'

'Could you tell me his address.'

Angel had no hesitation.

'No, we couldn't.'

She pointed at Spuggie who had also just entered the gate and was coming up the drive.

'But his sister Spuggie might. Come on, Jemma, we're late, let's run.'

And with that they were haring off.

As they ran past Spuggie, Jemma yelled out. 'That bloke wants to see you.'

And Angel added. 'Watch him, he's weird! Got a side parting!'

Spuggie stopped where she was, Lee came back to join her.

'You Fraser's sister?'

She nodded.

'Your mam still in hospital, is she?'

'Yes – and what's it to you?'

Lee smiled his nasty little smile.

'Just checking what you know.'
'Know?'
But he wasn't intent on answering questions.
'Tell Fraser he owes me; and funds are short.'
'Owes you for what?'
'I won't tell you now, but tell Fraser if he doesn't come up with the money, I'll tell you next time.'
'Tell me what?'
'Why not ask Fraser?'
And with that he was walking back to the gate, calling over his shoulder as he went.
'How do I get to be a member of this place?' Spuggie had it in a flash.
'You don't. It's for nice kids.'
He laughed and went through the gate just as Geoff was driving in.

Geoff pulled up alongside Spuggie, and wound the window down.
'So who was that one?'
'Who knows, Geoff. But maybe Fraser's got an idea.'
'Fraser?'
'Sorry, thinking out loud. Give us a lift as you're here, would you?'
Without waiting for his agreement, she opened the door and started getting in.
'Lazy beggar!'
She smiled as she said it, settling into her seat.
'Don't forget, Geoff – I'm the sister of the man who saved your life.'
Geoff said it heartfelt as he started driving on.
'Great! That's all I need! Spuggie getting in on the act as well!'

Later that afternoon, the scheme that had been on the boil since the morning came to fruition.
It was Lisa's idea, Donna had asked PJ, and PJ had pulled it off and got permission from the people who ran the outfit.
Now all three of them were at the local radio station all ready

to make the broadcast that hopefully would get Polly dashing home once more.

Donna was in the glass booth with headphones on, all ready to go on the red light, and on the other side of the glass, PJ and Lisa smiled their encouragement.

When it was time for it, Donna's message was simple and to the point.

'If you can hear me, Mam, please get in touch. You see, dad's had an accident. I mean he's not going to die, but they've found something else wrong as well. And I need your permission to . . . do something; so he doesn't have to spend all his life suffering.'

The message was simple, but Donna was fighting tears all the way. She succeeded in keeping them at bay until the broadcast was over, but when Donna came out of the cubicle, she fell into Lisa's arms sobbing, much to PJ's embarrassment.

One of the station reporter's hanging around, asked PJ what it was all about, and when PJ told him what Donna wanted to do, donate a kidney to her dying father, the man raised his eyebrows in amazement.

And PJ realised he'd given the man quite a story. He hoped there wasn't too much of a fuss made, or Donna might give him it in the neck for letting the cat out of the bag.

If he'd known then how big the story was finally going to be, he would have run for cover at once.

That evening Fraser heard Lou say to Spuggie that she couldn't talk to him as he was resting on doctor's orders. Being Spuggie of course she popped her head in in any case when Lou was busy somewhere else, but when she called his name he feigned sleep.

Fraser had made his mind up as to what he would do. He was going to fight his fear, and finally go into Cardboard City and find his mum, and if possible get her out to safety. He waited until he was sure everyone had gone to sleep, before getting up and dressed, then he crept out of the house without a sound. A long and hard cycle ride soon had him back on the bridge looking down on the area.

Fires still burned down there, and in their flickering light, drunks could still be seen meandering, but, tying his bike up to a bollard, Fraser put his fear behind him, and walked down the path into the nightmare world below.

A bottle smashed and a drunkard cursed nearby but he couldn't see where he was. An old woman weeping bitterly put her hand out to him plaintively as he passed, he gave her what change he had and pushed on towards the first of the cardboard dwellings. From nowhere a slobbering drunk was coming at him intent on grabbing him, but Fraser, his heart racing, ducked under the man's grasp, and thrown off balance the man staggered and fell. Fraser went on.

Soon he was opening boxes and looking at the usually sleeping inhabitants. Every face he saw was weary, and woe stained. It wasn't just old people. There were young boys and girls there as well, even younger than himself.

Opening one box, Fraser was amazed to see a young woman sleeping with three young children beside her. One of them woke and reacted frightened by Fraser's presence. Saying 'It's okay. Don't be frightened.' Fraser quickly moved on.

For more than an hour Fraser searched, and then knew that soon he must give up. The sights he had seen had depressed him so much, that he knew he would be scarred with this memory for life, and would never walk past another beggar without giving. It was no longer important whether it was their own fault they were in this predicament or not, they were in it, and needed all the help they could get.

Opening one box, he saw the person had their back to the opening, Fraser let the lid fall without disturbing them. Then as he moved away he heard the person turn. He walked back and opened the lid once more.

He saw that it was his mother, fast asleep.

Fraser knelt by the box, and looked at her. Her face, lit by the moonlight, had the look of an innocent child. Finally he spoke, gently.

'Mam.'

She made a slight movement but didn't wake. He said it again a little louder.

'Mam!'

Her eyes were immediately wide open, frightened, but then,

her eyes adjusting to the light, she saw who it was, recognised him, and spoke, clearly and brightly.

'Why, Fraser, love – what is it?'

And with the unexpectedness of the recognition, and the normality of the question in such squalid surroundings, Fraser was immediately too choked to reply, and fighting to keep his tears at bay.

'Can't you sleep, pet?'

Fraser shook his head for 'No'.

And then, as she had done a hundred times when he was a child she repeated the old formula.

'Well, you can get into the bed this time, son, but you mustn't make a habit of it. You're getting to be a big boy now. Come on, in you get, but quiet, don't want to wake your Da now, do we?'

And Fraser, accepting the invitation of her open arms, carefully climbed into the box and lay down alongside her, and as his mother folded her arms around him, and cuddled him to her, she spoke the words that finally cracked Fraser's resolve not to cry.

'There, there. You're safe now, pet. You go back to sleep, Fraser, love, no more nightmares now.'

And with that, his tears were flowing, and Fraser thought they would never ever stop.

CHAPTER SEVEN

As soon as dawn light had broken into her room, Spuggie, who had hardly slept a wink all night, was up and off to Fraser's room, all ready to give him a good cross-questioning. On flinging his door open, she was shocked to see that his bed was empty and obviously hadn't been slept in.

There was only one thing for it, time to consult Lou.

Opening that bedroom door the first thing that struck Spuggie was the snoring of Lou's other half, buried in the duvet beside her. Spuggie reckoned it would take an age to wake Lou if she could manage to sleep through that racket, but one touch of her shoulder and the whispered words, 'Wake up, Lou', and she was wide awake and seeing it was Spuggie was immediately alert and ready to give whatever help was needed.

'What is it, pet?'

'Fraser's gone. Been out all night.'

Lou sat up, and looked at the clock.

'How'd you make that out? He was in bed when we all went off – maybe he's just made an early start.'

Spuggie had the answer ready.

'I've been awake half the night, waiting till it was a reasonable sort of time before I could go in and talk to him. He's not there, and there was no noise of him going out.' Lou said it gently.

'He's a big boy, Spuggie, don't go worrying yourself.'

The retort was quiet angry.

'He's a big kid more like.'

Then Spuggie went on, expressing her real fear.

'I think he's in some trouble, Lou. There was this weird-looking bloke up at the Grove yesterday . . . '

'Weird?'

' . . . had a side parting, that's always considered a bit dodgy these days. Anyway, he said Fraser owed him some money.'

'For what?'

'He wouldn't tell me. But he said he *would* tell me if Fraser doesn't cough up – so it's obviously something bad.'

That gave Lou pause for thought. It was a blackmailer's line, and she didn't like it, but didn't want Spuggie to see her worry.

'You go back to bed now, Spuggie – I'll have words with him tomorrow.'

'But where is he?'

'He'll be somewhere safe, never fear.'

And Lou settled down once more as Spuggie headed for the door. Reaching it she turned back.

'You won't tell him I was worried, will you?'

Lou smiled her gentlest smile.

'Don't worry, Spuggie – your secret's safe with me.'

Spuggie looked once more at the bulky shape in the bed beside Lou.

'How do you manage to sleep through that racket?'

'Years of practice, pet.'

And with that Spuggie went. Only then did Lou's face show the anxiety she felt. Where had Fraser been all night?

In spite of the early hour the residents of Cardboard City were on the move. The reason was that on that day, the corporation cleaners were there with water cannon to hose the area and if not clean it, at least move the filth about a bit.

All unaware Fraser slept on, until he felt the box being kicked and the lid dragged open to allow the sun to pour in. He saw a figure standing there, the sun shining brightly behind them.

'That you, Mam?'

But it wasn't. As the person moved on to kick other boxes and ensure their tenants were also up and out, Fraser saw it was one of the workmen. For a fractional moment he couldn't understand where he was and why he was there in the first place, and then it all came flooding back. In a sort of frenzy Fraser swung to look at the other half of the box. It was empty. His mother had gone again. For a moment longer he sat there musing and gently scratching at an itch, then decided it was time to go home.

Arriving back on the bridge, he found his bike had been stolen.

At that point all over England newspaper boys and girls were busily delivering the various Sunday papers, and the ones who delivered the tabloids soon got sick of the face of the sad-faced girl who was on the front page of all of them.

It was Donna. And there were a variety of headlines, but the sharpest two said it in only three words each, 'Come home, Mam!' said one, and the other had 'Donna the donor'. After the first telephone call from another newspaper at six-thirty, Lisa without telling Donna what it was all about, left the telephone off the hook, and Donna all unknowing slept blissfully on.

An hour or so later, something soft landed on Debbie's bed and she awoke with a start. Her teddy was beside her rather than being on the floor where it usually ended up. She looked to Jemma's bed, and saw that she was bundled up and totally covered by the blankets so it couldn't have been her. Then it struck her. Jemma was still in bed! With that she was up and heading for the bedroom door at the double calling as she went.

'Beat you to it, Jemma!'

And for once she had. She slammed and locked the bathroom door behind her and was thrilled to be the first in there for once. But the thought of the strange arrival of teddy came back to mind. Jemma wouldn't . . .

With that she went past the small wicker dirty-clothes basket to fling open the tall airing cupboard door in the corner. It was empty. Deciding she was being foolish she went back to look at herself in the mirror. She decided she looked quite pretty today. Tried putting her hair up to see how it would look, and while it was up practised a few rather sexy smiles in the mirror at an imaginary dishy guy.

While doing so she noticed the small pimple at the side of her nose. With that she let her hair fall and opened the bathroom cabinet to get two bits of cotton wool from the large ball in there, to give it a squeeze.

She was so intent on doing it that she didn't see the lid of the wicker basket start to wobble. The reason it wobbled soon became clear. It was perched on Jemma's head, and Jemma oh-so-slowly was standing up in the wicker basket her arms hidden behind her, and her face gleaming with pleasure at having caught Debbie out so well. When she had fully stood, and just as Debbie was about to perform the operation on the spot she shouted it out loud:

'Don't pick your pimples!!'

And with the shock of it Debbie jumped in the air and then screamed.

In the bedroom, Angel laughing, rose from the made up bed on the floor where she had been sleeping overnight, and without using her arms which were also hidden behind her, went to Jemma's bed, and using her teeth, pulled out the pillow that was making the shape that had fooled Debbie into thinking that Jemma was still in there, and put it back in its proper place.

Spuggie was by then sitting with her chess set on her knee. It's red light was blipping on and off telling her it was her move, but she wasn't paying it any attention, her mind miles away.

But then, seeing Fraser arrive at the far corner of the green on foot, she was up and away and running for the front door.

Fraser was also in a bit of a dream, thinking over the happenings of the last few days, and only came from his reverie when a figure of whom he had been vaguely aware was running in his direction, came to a sudden halt a few metres in front of him. He saw who it was.

'Hi, Spuggie.'

With that, totally unexpectedly, she was running full at him, and without a word started kicking and pummelling him around the body.

He shouted as he tried to stop the blows landing.

'What you playing at! Don't be crazy! Pack it up, Spuggie!'

And then Spuggie was shouting equally loudly.

'I hate you, Fraser!! I really, really hate you!!' The words pouring out as she went on pummelling.

'How could you do that to me!! To me of all people! You could have been dead or anything!!'

Finally Fraser got her hands held and managed to contain her, just at the moment she burst into tears. Fraser was worried, this wasn't like her.

'What is it, Spuggie?! What's got into you?!'

The struggle went out of her as she said it through her tears.

'You're all I've got, Fraser! I thought you were gone!'

Fraser was touched. He knew she liked him really, but to actually say it was something else again. He let go of the hold he had on her before saying it.

'I wouldn't go without you, now would I? You're all I've got as well.'

She looked at him intently.

'You promise?'

Fraser smiled.

'Course I promise.'

And for a fractional moment she looked at him again to make sure he meant it, and then seeing that he did, started punching and kicking at him once more.

'Don't ever do owt like that again ever! You hear me!! Don't do it!!'

And for all the damage that was being done Fraser had to laugh. It's really nice to know you are loved.

'I hear you, Spuggie!! I hear you!'

In the living room of the Gallaghers', Robert had been coolly watching the battle on the green. Speedy passing through had also looked out to see what was going on, and then, as the fight on the green finally ended, noting Robert's sad face, decided to go for a peace pact.

'Going to the Grove tonight?'

Robert turned to look at him, surprised he had spoken. He didn't reply. Speedy, not to be put off so easily, enlarged on it.

'PJ's suggested that everybody who's going to do a turn, turns up and tries it out like.'

The remark came bitterly.

'You think I'm likely be doing a turn, aye, Speedy? Couple of handstands maybe? Followed by the splits?'

Speedy decided to battle on in spite of Robert's ill-temper.

'We're meeting with Charlie to practise a new song. She'll sing it tonight. Thought you might like to hear it.'

'We?'

'Me and Danny Dimmoro. Meeting at Dimmoro's café.'

Robert's remark carried a sneer.

'The pretty boy?'

And now, his new friend being unfairly picked on, Speedy was rankled.

'He's a nice kid and a mate of mine. Don't knock him when you don't know him, right?'

Robert turned and started moving off as he spoke.

'I think I'll manage to live without hearing Charlie sing your song, so I'll give it a miss.'

'That's good.'

Speedy's remark stopped him in his tracks. He turned back to look at him, and Speedy let him have it.

'Be a pity to put a damper on the evening before it's even started.' And pleased, Speedy saw he had scored the point.

There was an old broken bench halfway between the green and Gallaghers' and Fraser and Spuggie squeezed up together on the good half of it, as she got the cross-questioning underway.

'So how come you owe him money?'

'It's nothing, Spuggie. He's just a beggar boy, did me a favour.'

'A beggar boy?'

'That's right. He begs in the underpass near the pictures. Every morning before school and at lunch times.'

Fraser chuckled at the thought.

'He wears raggy clothes and then changes into his uniform before going in.'

Spuggie was appalled.

'That's a cheat.'

'Reckon you're right, but . . . that's life.'

Spuggie pressed on with it.

'So – what's the favour he did for you?'

Fraser shifted a bit and had a scratch.

'Nothing much.'

In a perfect echo of his body language Spuggie scratched herself in the same spot.

'Like what?'

Fraser had had enough. Spuggie's questioning was getting too close for comfort.

'Aw, come on, Spuggie, let it go, you're coming on like a jealous wife.'

'Just tell me what he did and I'll let it go.'
'I asked him to find where this woman lived, that's all.'
'A woman?!'
'That's right.'
'And did he?'
'Did he?'
'Find where she lived?'
'Yes – more or less.'
Fraser was relieved when Spuggie went off on a different tack.
'That's where you've been all night, isn't it! You've been in bed with a woman!'
'Don't be stupid! It was the far side of town, got late, she said I could sleep there, that's all.'
'You didn't do owt, did you?'
'No, no. She's not that sort of a person. I just slept there that's all.'
And with that, as Spuggie made her next remark, they both scratched delicately and in perfect harmony.
'Lucky for you. There's all sorts of things going round these days; besides which if our Mam found out she'd really give you what for.'
The itch having gone, the scratching was ended.
'So – best we don't tell her then, aye?'
Spuggie smiled.
'It'll cost you.'
Fraser was bemused.
'What?'
'About time you took me to the pictures again.'
In a split second Fraser was reliving the nightmare of their previous visit to the cinema. His mother was in his mind begging in the underpass; then she was in the cardboard box inviting him in to sleep.
Spuggie was alarmed at what she saw.
'What is it, Fraser? Fraser – what is it?'
He said the word softly.
'Nothing.'
'There's a tear rolling down your cheek.'
He wiped it away.
'It's nothing.'

And then to Spuggie's amazement, Fraser was in floods of silent tears, his body being racked by sobs that he fought to contain. She watched a moment, then unable to stop herself she cuddled him to her, saying the comforting words as she rocked him gently backwards and forwards.

'There, there ... it's going to be all right; it's going to be all right, Fraser, pet.'

But the tears continued to pour.

About the same time as Spuggie and Fraser finally headed for the house after Fraser's tears had subsided, Alan Dobson walked into the kitchen at the Dobsons', and was stopped dead in his tracks by the sight he saw. Angel and Jemma were eating their breakfast cereal, which was ordinary enough, but it was how they were doing it that gave Alan pause. They both had their arms behind their backs, and they each had a bare foot on the table, and their spoons were clutched between their big toe and second toe, and they were stretching forward, trying to eat the flakes off their spoons.

Alan's voice brooked no disobedience.

'Enough.'

It was Jemma who spoke having managed to get a mouthful without dropping too many flakes on the table.

'But we've only just started eating, Dad!'

'No enough of this stupidity. Enough of this project stuff. Your teacher should have more sense than let you get up to this sort of thing at weekends.'

Angel piped in.

'Oh, it wasn't Miss.'

'It wasn't?'

And Jemma finished it for her.

'No, it's our idea. Thought we'd try everything just to see which was the worst.'

'And?'

'And what?' said Jemma.

Alan spelt it out.

'Well you've been blind, you've been deaf, you've been legless, and now you're apparently armless; which is the worst?'

They spoke it together.

'Being deaf.'

'How'd you make that out?'

Angel started it.

'When people can see you've got a problem they help out . . . '

And Jemma finished it.

' . . . But when you're deaf they just treat you as if you're stupid.'

And having got the answer, Alan, in spite of their protests, put a stop to the project once and for all.

He demanded their feet were taken off the table, and that they went back to eating their food like normal non-disadvantaged kids. And being honest, in spite of their continued grumbling, they were pleased to do so.

Meanwhile Lou was giving a slightly hangdog Fraser a dressing down as he stood with Spuggie in the kitchen at the Gallaghers' having an occasional scratch.

'You were supposed to be in your sick bed, Fraser.'

He had the answer in a flash.

'I got sick of being in me bed, Lou.'

'Glib but not good enough. What's it all about?'

Fraser was just a pace behind Spuggie and with a nod he indicated to Lou he would tell her when Spuggie was out of earshot. Meanwhile Spuggie was giving her version of his story, while having a scratch at her head.

'He's been off sleeping at some woman's house, Lou, but we're not going to tell Mam 'cos she'll go mad.'

'I'm not exactly thrilled myself.'

And with that Fraser was going at his head as well, and Lou didn't miss the stereophonic scratching.

'What's got into you both with all this scratching?'

It was Fraser who said it for them both.

'Don't know, Lou. Something's driving me crazy.'

Lou crossed to Fraser.

'Pull your sleeve up, Fraser.'

He did so, and Lou saw the tell-tale red bite marks.

'Fleas! Don't know where you been, Fraser, but you are crawling.'

Spuggie still scratching was furious.

'Oh Fraser, how could you! Fancy sleeping at someone's who had fleas!'

Lou wasn't finished.

'Let's have a look at your head, Fraser.'

Spuggie was totally aghast.

'Not nits as well!!'

Fraser having bowed his head, Lou was looking and in seconds it was confirmed.

'Dead on the button, Spuggie.'

Spuggie was furious.

'Fraser, how could you do this to me!'

Lou went to the cupboard and got two large black plastic bags.

'Right, the pair of you. Strip off. Everything in there. Then into the bath. I'll put the anti-lice stuff on while you're in there.'

'But it stinks, Lou!'

'You think I don't know that, Spuggie, the years I've been looking after kids?'

Fraser was suitably apologetic.

'Sorry about this, Lou.'

Spuggie chipped in, peeved.

'What about me?'

In spite of the seriousness of the situation, Fraser still managed a smile.

'Teach you not to be soppy, won't it. This is what comes from cuddling brothers.'

And Spuggie tried to have the last word.

'This is what comes from staying out all night with manky women!'

But Lou beat her to it.

'Right. Shut the gabbing and away the pair of you go.'

Donna's mother Polly had put as much distance as she could between her and her ex-boyfriend. Now in a little seaside town down south, she was slowly recovering from the affair. She'd been there just long enough to start being a familiar figure, so when she went in the paper shop to buy her paper that morning, the man behind the counter felt he could ask the question when she reacted strangely to the sight of the tabloids spread on the shelf.

'What is it, love?'

Polly pointed at the picture on the front page.

'That's my daughter.'

He was impressed.

'And are you going to "Come home, Mum"?'

'With Donna, first you ring.'

And she had rung, often. And always got engaged. So the decision was finally made for her. If she wanted to know the details, she had to get in her car and make the long drive north.

From the moment that Lisa had woken Donna with a cup of tea, and told her that she was featured in the papers, and then put the phone back on the hook it hadn't stopped ringing. Newspapers and television for interviews, family for news of Jim, people who thought they had spotted Polly, and of course Nicola, who couldn't get through.

Having tried for the umpteenth time Nicola called her goodbyes to the family, and set off for the pub. Alan had drawn her attention to the front page, and Nicola wanted to find out what Donna was playing at making her dad's illness so public.

Lisa, took yet another call as she went downstairs to check the bar.

'Hello? ... Yes, she does – just a minute.'

Lisa crossed to the stairs and called up. 'Another reporter, Donna!'

Donna called back from the distance.

'I'll take it up here.'

She took the call and yet another interview was fixed in a trice. Putting the telephone down she thought about her reaction to the calls.

On the one hand she hated herself for feeling so chuffed that she was suddenly in the limelight. She realised now what the reporter at the radio station had been up to when he got her to pose for a photograph before she left, particularly asking her to look as sad as she could, which hadn't been difficult. She hated herself but, if she was going to get in touch with Polly what better way was there? The telephone rang again, and she took the call, not realising that at that very second Polly was also yet again calling, and getting engaged.

Meanwhile a worried PJ, travelling along at a wobble on his unicycle, using the shoulder of Duncan as a handy prop, was breaking the news to him about his involvement in the affair of front page Donna. Duncan was suitably comforting.

'I wouldn't worry about it, man. Donna'll love it.'

PJ had to admit he had a point, and went on to more serious matters, that night's try-out of the acts at Byker.

'So what you going to do then, Dunc? Saw Angel and Jemma in half again?'

'I can't – the coffin's in two halves.'

'Geoff'll make you a new one.'

'He won't – he was furious.'

'How come?'

'I took it to him and he said: 'You've sawed me coffin in half! it was a brand new one, and you've sawed it in half.'''

'It was a gag, man! You know what Geoff's like, it was just a gag.'

'Seemed serious enough when he said it.'

'Well, isn't there another trick you can do?'

'Yeh, but I'll need your help.'

'Well as long as you don't want me in fishnet tights and a blond wig parading with a placard, I'm your man.'

'Got to get in the cellar at the Grove on the quiet.'

PJ smiled.

''as that ever proved a problem before?'

And of course it didn't.

At Dimmoro's café Speedy and Danny's thoughts were also with the show. They wanted to try out a new song. Trouble was without their singer it was no easy trick. It was Danny who paused in his tinkling at the piano to say it.

'So where is she?'

Speedy let the sexist line slip out without a second thought.

'Who can tell with women? Play the tune again, Danny.'

Danny played it while Speedy checked the piece of paper he was holding. Speedy was pleased. As Danny stopped playing he said it with a smile.

'Okay – got it. Fits.'

And with that the door to the café opened and Charlie was flying in.

'Hi! Sorry I'm late. Trying to get through to Donna all morning – with you in a sec.' And with that she was heading for the telephone in the far corner.

Danny and Speedy's exchanged glance said it all: 'Women.'

It didn't take more than a few seconds to confirm the telephone was still engaged. Charlie slammed it down and crossed to them.

'Amazing! She's living on the phone at the moment.'

Flinging her coat down she addressed her remark at Speedy.

'So, what we got today?'

He passed her the latest lyric, 'Out of Tune With Your Heart', which she read through at speed as he watched her read. Speedy wondered as she did so, how she would feel if she knew that this song was a heartfelt plea from him to her. She smiled as she finished reading.

'Makes a nice change from "tuppenny daydreams."'

And all three just had to laugh.

The reason Charlie could not get through was not that Donna was on the telephone. The phone was now off the hook, so she could have a good bawling match with Nicola without being disturbed.

Within minutes of arriving, Nicola had made the accusation that Donna was serving her own ends by arranging to have her picture in the paper.

Donna had tried to put her straight.

'I didn't try to get my picture in the paper, it just happened through a reporter at the radio station!'

'You shouldn't have let them do it, Donna.'

'How could I stop them! Besides, whatever it costs to get Polly here and talking, I'll do it.'

Nicola was now really angry. Donna she thought was being incredibly thick.

'You're making Jim out to be a creep, as if he really would let his daughter donate a kidney like that.'

'Well why not!'

'You really can't see it, can you?'

'No! Tell me! What am I doing that is so wrong?'

Nicola spelt it out.

'Because what you're saying is going to happen isn't going to happen so it's all wrong you should say it in the first place.'

Donna flushed with anger.

'Who says it's not going to happen?'

'I do!'

'I'll prove you wrong – right?'

Nicola couldn't let it go.

'No father in his right mind would let his daughter do such a thing!'

Donna, terrified that Nicola might be right, screamed it loudly as if to convince herself.

'He will! If the choice is being on a machine for life or letting me do it he will!'

Nicola spoke very softly.

'I don't think you know Jim at all.'

And Donna's sarcasm was boundless.

'And you do, I suppose.'

At that moment Lisa arrived at the doorway and looked from one to the other before speaking.

'Camera crew outside, television. They want to do a news piece.'

Nicola looked at Donna as if willing her not to do it. Donna saw the look but ignored it. 'I'll just sort me make-up out and be with them in a second.'

Nicola picked up her bag, and swept past Lisa heading for the stairs.

Lisa's look asked Donna the question.

'She just doesn't understand that's all.'

Arriving at the Grove, Duncan and PJ had managed to get past

Geoff and Alison and into the cellar without any bother. The door had been locked, but it had only taken Duncan about ten seconds to sort that out as usual. Now Duncan was on a crate searching the ceiling for what he was looking for, while PJ was directing the torch they had brought with them in whatever direction Duncan asked him to.

Above their heads they could hear Geoff walking back and forwards into the main room, as he was busily setting up a small stage and curtains for the rehearsal night. Every time they heard him come through the room they stopped what they were doing and didn't speak. When he went Duncan continued the search, PJ was getting impatient.

'Are you sure about this, Duncan?'

'Yeh. I promise you there's one here somewhere.'

Duncan moved the box to another position and finally found what he was looking for.

'Great, that's it! No problem!'

What Duncan had discovered was a bolted and hinged flap, a trapdoor into the room above. Through it he intended to make Jemma and Angel disappear during the show. He opened the bolts to make sure they would come free, as PJ was speaking.

'You can't expect them to come through with nothing to land on?'

Duncan jumped down.

'We'll get the old mattress from the corner.'

And then as good as his word he went and got it, and pulled it under the trap.

'Hadn't you better bolt it up again?'

'We'll just check above, when Geoff packs up meandering, make sure it opens.'

And at that moment they heard Geoff's footsteps in the room above once more, and realised with a panic he was heading for the spot where the trap was.

At the same moment they realised it, there was a scream, and suddenly Geoff was shooting downward through the trap and landing on the mattress at their feet. Duncan spoke first.

'We'll cancel the check, PJ, it obviously still works.'

And as Geoff, totally bemused, looked round saying, 'What the 'eck!' PJ greeted him cheerily.

'Hello, Geoff man, nice of you to drop in.'

As Donna went to face the three-man television crew, having forgotten to put the telephone back on its cradle, Polly was coming out of a telephone kiosk for the fourth and last time. She was on the main road and decided she wouldn't pause to make any more useless calls, simply go straight there. As she drove off she didn't see what she left behind her as she pulled away, the same substance she had left unknowingly behind her at every other stop.

It was a small pool of oil. It would have taken a forensic unit to tell what type of oil it was and what it was used for, but the answer would have been; brake fluid.

As Donna started to speak her simple message straight into camera with Lisa looking on from the doorway, Polly drove on.

'All I want is for me mam to get the message and get in touch.'

As she spoke the words, Polly breasted a steep hill.

'There are those who say what I'm trying to do is stupid.'

And as Polly, rolling downwards, started gathering speed, she eased her foot on the brake pedal and getting no response she too spoke quite quietly.

'No.'

She continued to pump at the brake pedal progressively firmly.

'... But I think when I've talked it through with Mam she'll say yes.'

And as Donna said 'yes' Polly for the first time screamed.

'No!'

The traffic below Polly was in a static jumble as Donna spoke on.

'I know I'll have to get Dad's permission as well – but I'll face that when I come to it ... '

And as Polly, now going at breakneck speed, realised the inevitable was to happen, she screamed long and loud as if in answer to Donna's request.

'So – if you hear this, come home, mam, just ... come home.'

'Nnoo!!'
'That's all I ask . . . come home!'
'Nnnnnoooooo!!!!'

And at that exact moment Donna felt as if she had been punched in the heart, the breath rushed out of her, one giant gasp, and unable to stop herself, knees buckling beneath her, she was sitting on the doorstep. Lisa was quickly at her side.

'What is it, Donna?'

Donna was both dazed and bemused.

'I dunno. Just felt really weird.'

And then to her horror she knew what it was.

She turned to Lisa, her face drained white with fear.

'I think something bad's happened.'

'To who?'

Tears stung Donna's eyes.

'It's Mam. She's dead, Lisa. I just know she's dead!'

And Donna ran inside the house, tears streaming, and the crew knew without being told that the interview was at an end.

CHAPTER EIGHT

Fraser and Spuggie sat side by side wrapped in big bath towels as Lou none too gently massaged the pongy lice remover into both their heads. As Lou finished having a final go at hers, Spuggie's comment was heartfelt.

'You know, Fraser, I'll never forgive you for this.'

'I think I've got the message, Spug.'

But he really had other things on his mind.

'How long before I can go and see Geoff, Lou?'

Lou carried on finishing off his hair as she spoke.

'Give it half an hour and you can be on your way.'

Spuggie pricked up her ears at the mention of Geoff.

'What do you want to see him for at this time of day?'

'You know, Spuggie, I must be the only bloke who knows why marriages fail without having to go to the bother of getting married first to find out.'

She was suitably thrown by the unexpectedness of the remark.

'Why?'

'Too many blinking questions!'

And as Spuggie gave a delighted chuckle at the thought, Lou also finished Fraser's hair, and told them both they could go get dressed again.

In the Grove office, Geoff had intended to give PJ and Duncan a severe dressing down, but they were as set on convincing him of the need for the course of action they had taken. Duncan having pleaded the case once, PJ was trying to reinforce it by saying exactly the same thing again, only moving the words around a bit so it looked like a different argument.

'Yeh, but can't you see, Geoff man, Duncan's right, if we'd asked permission, you would've had to ask what we were up to, and the trick would be spoilt for you tonight, right?'

But Geoff was having none of it.

'Instead of which I end up doing a swallow dive through the floorboards, and landing on me butt.'

Duncan persevered, this time trying to get Geoff onto a different tack.

'The good thing is, Geoff, now you do know, would you mind helping out tonight?'

Geoff seeing what was going on, was suitably staggered at the sheer neck of them both.

'You're supposed to be both on the carpet and being told off for being in the cellar *and* almost breaking me neck! Not trying to turn me into a magician's assistant!'

Duncan dismissed the thought.

'Naw – the job's not that posh, Geoff. Just opening up the trap at the start of me act, and then locking it again after. Would you?'

'You forget, Duncan, audition night, I've got to be there watching to see if it's any good.'

PJ had the answer to that one.

'No, Geoff. You're weeks ahead of yourself. None of the stuff's polished or owt, this is just a first gander to see what everybody's getting up to. I mean let's face it, I've hardly learned how to fall off me unicycle yet.'

Duncan couldn't resist that one.

'Oh I don't know, PJ. I thought you were falling off it really well.'

And Geoff, in giving a chuckle, knew he'd lost the battle.

The rehearsal night was as expected chaotic. Geoff had hung a curtain round the small raised dais where they were all to do their bit, and PJ as master of ceremonies, rode back and forward to the centre of the area on his unicycle opening and closing the curtain as he went. Everybody thought that was rather good, until realising that if he hadn't hung on to the curtain he would probably have fallen off his bike.

Danny had got the evening under way, playing a souped-up rendering of 'Come To The Cabaret' at the piano, and PJ having cycled the curtains open, Jemma and Angel were brave enough to kick it all off with a very short-lived display of juggling.

When everybody had finally collected all the balls from where they had landed around the room after Jemma slipped, and PJ had closed the curtains, there was a lot of banging and crashing back stage and then, after a big build up from PJ the curtain was re-opened, Winston, Kelly and the dog were there. The reason for the banging was obviously the setting up of the podium centre stage. The only trouble was the dog wouldn't stay on it. Each time they put him on it, he jumped straight back off again. Winston, losing his cool, was a sight to behold, and Kelly apologising because they didn't know the dog was scared of heights brought the house down. Strangely enough the whole business was probably funnier than the intended act would have been, and everybody simply roared with laughter as the battle of wills continued.

Speedy, sitting off in a corner with Charlie waiting for the time when she would sing, watched her laughing and felt his heart swell. She had said the song he had written, the one they had practised that day at Dimmoro's, was brilliant, and that was the one she intended to perform tonight.

Every time he saw her saying it in his mind's eye, he flushed with pride and pleasure. She didn't know it but it was their song. And then, remembering that Robert wasn't coming, his pleasure was complete.

The only one of the regulars who missed the fun was Donna. She had spent the day sitting in her room looking out of the window, and now watched the daylight slowly fade, hoping against hope that Lisa was right in what she had said. She had said that Polly would be fine. It was just the tension of being on television for the first time that had made Donna fall.

She had also gone on to tell a white lie. She had said the interviewer had told her that it often happened with people having their first interviews, but you never saw it on television because it was always cut out. This lie had later been confirmed when Donna saw herself on the early news, and the interview was cut off before she had sat.

But, why hadn't Polly come?

At that point Lisa came into her room, all ready with her coat on.

'I'm off to see Jim now, Donna, want a lift?'

Donna shook her head.

'I'll give it a while longer. See if she turns up.'

'Okay.'

Lisa was about to go when Donna spoke her inner thoughts out loud.

'Why doesn't she come, Lisa? She must have heard by now or seen the papers? Why doesn't she come?'

'I don't know, Donna pet. She may be out of the country, taking a holiday or something.'

'No. She would have rang me if it was anything big like that – have a good brag.' Donna thought about it before speaking. 'You know when I had that funny turn. I really did get the strangest feeling something had just happened to her.'

Lisa said it patiently.

'We promised not to talk any more about that, Donna.'

But Donna found it impossible to let it go so easily.

'I can't help it. What do I do if she's dead? How could I possibly handle that? It's just like Dad, I never got around to telling her I loved her. How could I handle it, Lisa?'

Lisa's smile was meant to be comforting.

'You won't have to – 'cos she's not. See you later.'

But Donna was not comforted. As Lisa left the room, she said it to herself quietly, while looking through the window into the encroaching gloom.

'How could I handle that?'

When Debbie and Tessa had finished their tap dance, and the next act was being set up, Spuggie had nipped off to the tea bar for a quick coffee. Just outside the office in the corridor, Fraser and Geoff were in earnest conversation. When he had been to the club that afternoon Fraser wouldn't tell her what it was all about, now unashamed Spuggie got into a position where she could eavesdrop unseen.

It was Geoff who was doing the chatting, keeping his voice down so they couldn't be overheard. Despite his efforts, bat-eared Spuggie heard every word.

'I've been in touch with the hospital. We've only got to get her there, and they'll clean her up and fix her up with a bed.'

Fraser was obviously pleased.

'Great, Geoff man!'

'Think nothing of it. Once this lot's cleared tonight and we've locked up, we'll go there in the car, and you can show me where she's at.'

'It's a bit rough.'

'Nothing we can't handle I'm sure.'

And having heard, Spuggie now knew what it was all about. The manky woman whose house Fraser had stayed in the night before was poorly, and Fraser was being a good Samaritan in sorting her out and getting her off to hospital along with Geoff. Spuggie decided then and there she would show them both that she was a good Samaritan herself, and unknown to either of them would go along and help out too.

She ducked back into the tea bar as PJ arrived at the run calling for Geoff as he came.

'Get a move on, Geoff man! Duncan's on!' And Geoff headed for the basement door as he called.

'On me way, PJ!'

Duncan was indeed on stage and taking it all very seriously. He had got a top hat and wand from somewhere. And Jemma and Angel were back on stage once more as his helpers. He made the announcement rather grandly.

'As you see, all I have for this demonstration of my magical art, is two halves of a well-sawed coffin.'

And true enough there were the two halves of the coffin he had sawed in two the day before, standing in front of him with their head holes uppermost.

'Plus, of course, my two charming young lady assistants.

There was general hooting at this description of Jemma and Angel. It was Debbie who shouted it through the furore.

'You wouldn't say that if you could see them at home in the bathroom, Duncan!'

But Jemma knew she could top that, and bawled it through the bedlam.

'Well if he saw what you get up to in there, our Debbie, it would put him off his breakfast for life!'

And as Debbie blushed red, there was yet more laughter at the sight.

Duncan finally calmed them down, and picked up a loop of bamboo cane which had some curtaining dangling from it.

'To continue. This curtaining goes over the coffins like so.'

He put the loop over the two coffin halves and laid it on the floor, everybody watching fascinated not knowing what was going to happen next. Having laid it down he took Jemma and Angel's hands and led them forward.

'Now my two assistants will climb onto the coffins.'

And holding his hand to steady themselves they did so. Then Duncan lifted the bamboo ring and standing at its centre said.

'I too will mount the coffin.'

And he did so. It was a bit of a crush but they were finally on.

'Now I would like you to count to ten as I raise the curtain to cover all three of us.'

Duncan started the counting then everybody picked it up and the noise was deafening. As they reached ten all three were out of sight behind the hanging cloth, and then Duncan dropped it, and there was a 'whoo!' of amazement followed by applause. Jemma and Angel were gone from where they had been standing and now their smiling heads were sticking through the holes in each coffin half. Duncan jumped down, retrieved the loop of bamboo and climbed back again.

'We count again.'

And once more the count was taken up by the audience, and at ten Duncan was again out of sight. This time when the curtain dropped, Jemma and Angel were standing on the boxes, and then as they leapt down and quickly turned the boxes out of the way, it could be seen that Duncan had totally disappeared. The applause at the brilliant trick was deafening.

In the basement Geoff was on his back poleaxed; he'd been glancing at his watch as Duncan had bulleted down and landed on the back of Geoff's neck, and the blow had knocked him flying. Now climbing off Geoff's back where he was resting comfortably, Duncan was worried at Geoff's lack of movement.

'Geoff man! Are you all right?!'

He need not have worried, Geoff rolled over to face him, he was still conscious but winded. He spoke angrily as he started to sit up.

'I was expecting delicate little lasses to drop through, not a big lump like you!'

Duncan remembered too late he hadn't told Geoff of the change of plan.

'Sorry. Changed the trick for a better one at the last minute.'

But at that Geoff was screaming 'Watch out!' at Duncan and pushing him to one side. And Duncan saw why. PJ's unicycle was flying through the hole, and a split second later with a yelp of fear, PJ was following suit.

He landed with a bump on the mattress, and then, quickly recovering looked at Geoff accusingly.

'You were supposed to bolt it up again, Geoff man!'

And it was about that moment that a furious Geoff decided that the show would definitely be cancelled.

At the hospital, Lisa, standing at the window in Jim's room, had been looking out at the night-time sky, wishing desperately that Jim would regain consciousness.

If she had glanced towards Jim's bed at that moment, she would have seen that her wish was being granted.

Once more Jim's eyelids flickered, but this time they opened and stayed open.

He looked round trying to work out where he was, then his head turned fractionally, and he saw Lisa standing at the window. He had to try it a few times before words came, but they finally did.

'Hi, Lisa.'

And thrilled Lisa turned from the window and saw that he was looking at her. She said it in a disbelieving whisper.

'Jim!'

And then she was running to his side, and embracing him. Then they gently kissed.

Finally Jim spoke again, his voice hoarse.

'How long have I been out?'

Lisa had to think about it.

'Seems like forever, but it's only a few days.'

Jim was amazed.

'As long as that?'

She nodded.

'I imagine you've been a bit worried.'

She had to smile at the understatement, and then understated it herself.

'You could say that, yes.'

He realised she was by herself.

'Donna?'

'She'll be along any time. Waiting for a phone call.'

Getting it wrong and thinking it was probably boyfriend stuff, Jim smile.

'That's my Donna.'

And seeing he had got it wrong, Lisa tried to put it right without giving the game away.

'She's been trying to contact Polly. She wants to . . . She's got a suggestion to make.'

Jim was perplexed.

'Suggestion?'

'I'll let her tell you herself.'

Donna was lying fully dressed on the bed when the telephone rang. She rushed hopefully to take the call.

'Hello! Oh it's you, Lisa.'

Her disappointment that it was Lisa and not Polly, turned to joy when Lisa broke the news about Jim coming round finally.

'Really! That's great news! I'm on my way now.'

Lisa asked if Polly had been in touch.

'No. Not yet. But I'll come in any case.'

And at that moment, Donna's bedroom was lit by a flashing blue light. She carried the telephone to the window, and her heart beat rapidly against her chest at what she saw.

She told Lisa in a frightened gasp.

'Lisa! There's a police car outside! . . . '

The car door opened and a policeman got out. ' . . . A policeman's coming to the front door! She's dead, Lisa! I just know Polly's dead!'

And with that Donna had slammed the telephone down and went running for the stairs, down them, then headed along the short corridor for the front door, and arrived there even before the bell was rung.

She swung the door open and faced the policeman.

'My mother?!'

And the policeman smiled at her.

'She's just coming.'

And he moved aside, and Donna saw that a policewoman had helped her mother from the back of the police car, and that Polly now stood there thanking her for her help.

Donna raced down the path to be at her side.

Polly spoke somewhat shakily.

'Hello, Donna. I've been in an accident but I'm okay. Police kindly brought me here. Sorry it took so long.'

And with that Donna was hugging her, and without being able to stop herself burst into floods of tears. Polly hugged her in return saying, 'There, there. It's all right now, pet. I'm here.'

Finally Donna managed to get the words out. Words that she had been desperate to say all day, and had thought she would never be able to say again.

'I love you, Mam! I really, really, love you!'

The moment Speedy had waited for all evening was upon him. Charlie was on stage, he was now sitting to one side of it, and Danny was playing the short introduction to the new song.

But when the introduction finished, Charlie didn't start singing. Danny looked at her surprised, and a whisper went round the room, as everybody realised something wasn't quite right.

Charlie was staring towards the entrance of the club. Speedy stood a little to see what she was looking at, and then having seen, he slumped back into his chair defeated.

Robert was standing in the doorway. He had decided to come after all.

Once more Danny played the introduction, and this time Charlie sang.

'How can you sing when you're out of tune,
Out of tune with your heart,
How can you sing when you've hurt your love,
By making a dream fall apart.'

And Charlie's eyes never left Robert's as she continued, and inside, Speedy's heart died a little with each word she sang.

'How do you play it,
How do you say it,
How do you say – Let's try again.
How can you sing when you're out of tune,
Out of tune with your heart.'

A deathly hush had settled over Byker, everybody realised this was an incredibly special moment. They almost held their breath, so as not to shatter its wonder. They knew Charlie had never sung so emotionally in her life, she was meaning every word.

How can you sing when your life's off key,
And you have nowhere to turn,
How can you sing when life's melody,
Makes your lonely hurt burn.

And then Speedy being so close was perhaps the first to notice, Charlie was crying. Her voice remained totally true, but as she sang the last verse she was crying.

'Major and minor, become as one,
When there's no one to share,
Living and dying are just the same,
When there's no one to care.'

And then Speedy saw she wasn't the only one. Both Angel and Debbie were rubbing tears from their eyes as Charlie finished.

'How do you say it,
How do you play it,
How do you say – Let's try again.
How can you sing when you're out of tune,
Out of tune with your heart.'

The music finally died away. And the silence seemed to hold and go on forever.

And then it broke and a roar of cheering, roaring and clapping was underway in a manner that Byker had never heard before, and in the middle of the mayhem, Speedy simply sat there silent, his heart he knew truly broken, and his love for

Charlie a heavy weight, that he knew, if he was to retain his sanity, he must finally put down.

After the applause had died away, and PJ having announced that the rehearsal was at an end, people started meandering off, but Speedy went on sitting lost in his thoughts.

'Speedy.'

The word broke through his musing and he looked up. It was Danny.

'That's a nice song. And she sang it well.'

Speedy looked to the far side of the room, to where Charlie and Robert hand-in-hand headed for the tea bar.

'Yeh. Trouble is she sang it at the wrong bloke.'

Danny saw where Speedy looked and finally realised why he was so down.

'Always the way, Speedy, always the way. Nobody ever sings songs for the songwriter.'

Speedy stood purposeful.

'Where you going? Tea bar?'

Speedy shook his head.

'Get a bit of fresh air.'

Danny watched him head for the front door, and then realised he had been joined by the two terrors. Angel was the first to speak, as if to make up for her emotional involvement in the song.

'Why does he always write such mushy songs?'

Danny had to smile.

'Maybe he's in love, Angel.'

But Jemma wasn't having that.

'Naw. People like Speedy don't fall in love.'

And Angel agreed.

'Be daft, wouldn't it? I mean who'd go out with a bloke like Speedy?'

And having passed judgement, they went off about their business.

In the tea bar, Charlie had guessed the truth as soon as she and Robert had sat down.

'You're going, aren't you?'

There was no way Robert could wrap it up, so he let her have it straight.

'Yes.'

'When?'

'Tomorrow. I'm here to say goodbye.'

'When will you be back?'

'I won't, Charlie. This goodbye's for good.'

'Just like that?'

Robert took a long time finding the right words.

'I love you, Charlie. Though you'd never have known it by the way I've been, I love you.'

She could see no logic to it.

'So why are you going?'

'Because ... I love you, Charlie, and you deserve better.'

'Maybe I don't want better.'

And then he told her the cold truth.

'I'll never know whether that's true or not, and that's what I can't live with.'

And she knew she had lost him for good.

He stood, said, 'See you,' and walked away.

And she didn't call him back again.

Speedy sat in the Grove grounds on the climbing frame and thought his thoughts. He heard the front door open, and then slam closed, but he didn't look in that direction. After a long time he realised someone was standing close by watching him. He looked. It was Robert. Uninvited he sat.

Finally he broke the silence.

'I'd thought you'd like to know that Charlie and I are through.'

Speedy had nothing to say to that.

'I know you keep her photograph in your room; and I saw the way you were looking at her in there.'

Speedy was too drained for this.

'And I saw the way she looked at you, Robert.'

Speedy stood ready to go.

Robert still intent on spelling out the message said it again.

'I'll be gone tomorrow. The field's clear.'

Speedy smiled, and then said it sadly.

'Naw, It's no good, Robert, Got to come to me senses finally. I'll always be just "Speedy" to her, and the sooner I come to terms with it the better.'

And with that he walked off, leaving Robert alone with his thoughts.

After listening patiently as Polly explained how her life had been saved by turning the car away from the jammed traffic below, and over the pavement, to end up travelling along a long, low hedgerow that acted, over its two or three hundred metre length as a brake, Donna finally found a gap in the conversation, and had managed to tell Polly why she wanted to get in touch with her so urgently.

Polly's first reaction was an instant 'No!' but Donna had verbally battled with her, until she won a begrudging agreement from her, which she now was explaining excitedly to Jim.

'It took a lot of convincing, Dad, but Polly finally agreed, so all you need to do is agree as well, and we can go ahead as soon as you're a bit better and do it.'

Jim was by then really tired, but fought against letting his eyes close.

'Somewhere along the line I've sort of missed what I'm supposed to be agreeing to, Donna.'

Donna was amazed.

'Didn't Lisa tell you?'

'No. Said you had a suggestion, that's all.'

Donna was pleased that Lisa had kept her secret, now she could have the pleasure of watching his eyes light up when she broke the news.

'I want to give you one of my kidneys, Dad.'

Jim's face immediately stiffened, a look of instant shock crossing it, and then it slowly softened, and Donna was amazed to realise he was chuckling.

'No wonder Polly said yes. She'd know I'd never agree to owt so daft.'

Donna was totally shocked at his choice of word.

'Daft?'

'That's right, pet. Daft. I'd not let you mar yourself, and disadvantage yourself like that for me, pet.'

Her dream of doing just one wonderful thing in her life was rapidly slipping away and she fought to hold on to it.

'But, Dad! ... '

But again he interrupted her. And she listened stony-faced to what he said.

'I'll give you the good news straight off so we can stop talking about it once and for all. Doctor was in less than half an hour ago. They've started to function again, Donna. Both of them, I won't be needing a kidney off anyone, and certainly not off my lovely little girl.'

And looking at her face he realised how much it had meant to her.

'But thanks for the offer, pet. It was very brave of you.'

Donna was fighting tears. Yes it was marvellous news. Her dad wouldn't need her kidney. Marvellous. But still she was fighting tears. He smiled at her gently.

'Now – isn't that wonderful news, pet?' She knew she must not cry no matter what. 'Yes, Dad ... that's wonderful news. Really, really wonderful.'

But she did cry. And Jim would always think it was joy, when in fact it was sheer heartbreak.

Spuggie was hidden in Geoff's car, lying on the floor in front of the back seats, and had covered herself with a rug she had found there. She had been in there since everybody had started leaving the club about fifteen minutes before, and waited patiently for Geoff and Fraser to arrive and get the journey underway.

When they had arrived, Spuggie held her breath as the back door of the car opened, but it was just Geoff throwing his briefcase on the back seat, and then he slammed the door closed again without spotting her, got in front with Fraser, and was soon driving away.

The journey seemed to take forever and Spuggie got progressively more uncomfortable as she was bumped about in the back. She reckoned Geoff must have hit every possible pothole in Newcastle. She was in fact about ready to give the game away by sitting up and declaring her presence, when a remark from Geoff, one of the very few he made during the journey, stopped her in her tracks.

'The good thing is, with a bit of luck, Spuggie need never know a thing about it.'

And Fraser's reply, 'Let's hope you're right.' Was so heartfelt that Spuggie decided to carry on hiding.

While she did so she wondered why seeing a sick old woman could be so bad for her. Finally, after what seemed like forever, the car came to a halt, the handbrake was applied, and the engine was switched off. But neither Geoff nor Fraser moved for a while, as if they were looking at something through the window, then she heard Geoff say it in a quiet, slightly awed voice.

'Ready for it?'

And Fraser agreeing equally quietly.

'Ready when you are.'

And with that she heard them both get out of the car and start walking away.

Spuggie waited till their footsteps had died away before she too sat up and looked out of the side window.

She had expected to be on some run-down grotty street, but she realised the car was parked on a bridge, and couldn't understand that. Stepping out of the car, and slamming the door behind her, she looked to see where Geoff and Fraser were going.

And as she caught sight of them, the full horror of where they all were struck home. Geoff and Fraser were walking down a pathway to hell.

Smoky fires by the dozen, were burning in the blackness below, and wild-looking scarecrow figures, male and female, lit by the flickering flames shouted and screamed at the two men as they descended into the area, waving their fists at them, mistaking them in their reasonably smart clothes for officials. Spuggie watched as Geoff and Fraser bravely walked on ignoring the mob. Spuggie knew she didn't have the courage to follow them down there. Couldn't possibly go into that dangerous filth-infested underworld. But even as she thought it, her feet working on automatic pilot, were walking her in the same direction. She knew something very serious was going on and she wanted to know the why of it.

If she thought it had been noisy above on the bridge, the sound that now battered her ears as she reached the vast cardboard box strewn wasteland, was horrendous. She could see two drunks fighting over a bottle in the distance, as they fought the bottle flew from their tugging grasp and smashed against an iron pillar emptying its contents to the dust, and they fought even harder. She skirted them, still trying to keep Fraser and Geoff in her sight, but they were moving ahead quickly and purposefully. She lost track of them as an old woman dressed in rags, stood crying and begging in front of her, blocking her view.

Spuggie screamed she had no money and ran past her, but Fraser and Geoff were now nowhere to be seen, and she suddenly felt very alone and frightened and vulnerable.

She started to run forward desperate to catch them up again, avoiding whatever trouble came her way as deftly as she could.

Drunks grabbing at her as she past proved no problem, they were much too far gone to be a real danger, but a small pack of wild-looking dogs who came out of the darkness to sniff at her, made her heart race and stopped her in her tracks, but they soon went on their way without attacking her. She looked back the way she had run, making sure no one was following her, and off to one side some way back, she saw Fraser and Geoff leaning over a cardboard box. She had overtaken them.

She crossed in that direction and hid behind another box about fifty metres from them so they wouldn't catch sight of her. There was a pile of rubber tyres blazing away near where they were, lighting up the scene and giving off dense clouds of acrid smoke that drifted over the area and hazed her sight.

They were helping someone out of the box they leant over, but the smoke wasn't allowing her to see who it was. Finally, as the box she was hiding against moved as someone turned in their sleep, Spuggie started moving in that direction. She kept going until she was about ten metres or so from them, and as they had their backs to her they didn't see her, and also hid the person from her view. She caught a glimpse between their shoulders as they gently helped the person to get out of the box, and Spuggie saw it was an old woman dressed in a shabby black coat pinned at the neck and waist with safety pins. With the glimpse she remembered Fraser talking to an old woman in the underpass, and thought maybe that's who he had decided to help.

Having got the woman safely out of the box, Fraser and Geoff turned in Spuggie's direction, supporting the woman between them, with a hand under each of her arms. Spuggie now could see that the woman's face, which was black with caked dirt, was startled, slightly frightened, not knowing what was going on.

Geoff and Fraser were walking her slowly and carefully over the rubble that was all around, and they walked towards Spuggie who simply stood her ground watching them. And then Fraser saw her first, followed by Geoff, and they both stopped walking. They were now only a few metres from Spuggie, and all three were well lit by the burning tyres, when Spuggie looked at the woman's face once again. And with a heart-jolting sense of horror and disbelief, for the first time she realised who it was.

Her mother.

Neither Fraser nor Geoff said a word, simply stood there and looked at Spuggie's horror stricken face, and watched as the tears slowly began to roll down her cheeks. When Spuggie finally got the words out, she spoke them with the incredibly contained anger of one who has been cheated of their rights.

'You should have told me, Fraser. You should have told me.'

But Fraser had nothing to say, and could only hang his head.

The woman, on hearing Spuggie's voice looked up, and her face which had been dead and non-comprehending, slowly started to come alive, as she looked intently at this girl in front of her who had spoken. And then, magically, it was as if dawn light had touched her, and lit her eyes inside with its glow. Slowly her face brightened, and finally a joyous smile came to her lips, and she spoke for the first time.

'I know you! You're Spuggie, aren't you?'

Spuggie knew she was crying. Knew her face was awash with disbelief at the pitiful sight she was seeing before her. But from somewhere deep inside, she found the words, found the ability to smile, and in the face of her mother's obvious joy at seeing her, smiled and said it.

'That's right, Mam. I'm Spuggie.'